**He grasped her arms
and spoke urgently.**

"If I am enga... when the c... Sutcliffe car... whatsoever, ... her choosing ... ...vered our relationship. So I am asking you to do me the favor of becoming my fiancée."

"No!" Jane shook her head vigorously. "No, it's impossible. You see, I'm m—"

"Why is it impossible, Jane?" Philippe's voice was suddenly tinged with hardness. "You've received letters in a man's handwriting, but you're obviously not engaged...."

Jane nodded automatically. "No, I'm n-not engaged."

"Then what is the obstacle?"

"Only the small matter of my marriage," she wanted to say, but the anguish of not being free to love this wonderful man made her hold back the words.

ANNE HAMPSON

château in the palms

Harlequin Books

TORONTO • NEW YORK • LOS ANGELES • LONDON
AMSTERDAM • PARIS • SYDNEY • HAMBURG
STOCKHOLM • ATHENS • TOKYO • MILAN

Harlequin Presents first edition October 1982
ISBN 0-373-10535-5

Original hardcover edition published in 1979
by Mills & Boon Limited

CHAPTER ONE

TENSION filled the air as the couple looked at one another. Jane's face, almost sallow in the saffron light from the wall lamp above her head, was twisted in anguish even while her soft brown eyes held an expression of protesting disbelief.

'You're—admitting it, Don? You're telling me it's true—— What you've j-just said?'

'I wouldn't have said it if it wasn't true,' he returned impatiently. 'I want my freedom. I've met someone else. I can't put it any plainer than that, can I?' He turned away, frowning. 'I've said I'm sorry, and that I don't want to hurt you——'

'Hurt me?' she broke in fiercely. 'You don't want to hurt me? What are you doing but hurting me? I love you, Don! I won't give you up to another woman! I *won't*!' She winced with pain as she heard the exclamation of anger that followed her protest.

'Fortunately divorce is simple these days,' he said. 'If you won't divorce me then I shall divorce you.'

She shook her head, tears streaming down her face. Fumbling for a handkerchief, she again protested, saying disjointedly that it wasn't true—it could not be true! They loved one another! His interest in this girl was nothing more than infatuation! Don knew this, surely he knew it.

'It can't be deep!' she cried, the sob in her throat causing her to stammer. 'It's m-me you—you l-love!

You can't break up our marriage for someone you've known for only a few months!'

'What has time to do with it? You and I hadn't known one another very long when we got married.'

Jane turned from him, the handkerchief to her eyes. He was right; it had been a whirlwind courtship, with Don, tall and fair and handsome, sweeping her off her feet and declaring he would not even consider the six-month engagement which Jane had wanted.

'You're too beautiful and tempting. I want you now!' He had taken her in his arms, crushing her to him, kissing her passionately. Her dark hair was like silk, he said, burying his face in it, her skin was soft as the petals of a milk-rose, her eyes gentle and trusting as a fawn's. Jane at eighteen had fallen madly in love with him, and for the past four years her life had been bliss. Orphaned at the age of six, she had been brought up by an aunt who had since died. She had been good to Jane but often over-strict.

'Marry in haste—you know the rest,' said her aunt warningly, but Jane followed the dictates of her heart, confident that the day would never dawn when she would regret it. But about three months ago Don had begun working late at the office, and once or twice recently he had told his wife that he was wanted at the firm's head office, which was more than two hundred miles away. Jane had thought it strange that his boss should send him off at a week-end, but Don was ready with a most convincing explanation which his trusting wife accepted without question. Yet, some-how, she was affected by nagging doubts as time went on. These doubts she managed to thrust away, admon-ishing herself for her suspicions. They were not really suspicions, but rather the merest threads of curiosity about the work which her husband was called upon to do. She had never questioned him, though. It would have been impossible to do so, simply because there was no substance in these threads of curiosity. Her seraphic innocence, her complete trust, her confidence in his loyalty ... all these had appealed to him, and in the beginning he would have been shocked if by some miracle he could have seen what he was to do to her in the future.

But this girl he had met three months ago had drawn him irresistibly by her voluptuous beauty, by her vivacious nature, her vitality and her experienced love-making. These things he admitted, as his wife stood there, her back to him, her shoulders drooping, her heart dying in excruciating agony within her.

'And so you see,' he told Jane finally, 'there's nothing left for you and me. I do love her, in spite of what you say, and I want to marry her. I hope, Jane, that you'll be sensible and stop acting as if we're the first people this sort of thing has happened to.'

'How can you be so heartless about it?' she cried, turning again to face him. 'These four years when we've been so happy together—sharing, loving—don't they mean anything to you?'

He sighed and frowned and shrugged his shoulders. 'The chapter's closed as far as I'm concerned, Jane. We're having a divorce, and that's my final word.'

It wasn't possible! This could not be happening—not to them—her and the husband she adored! No, it was a horrible nightmare....

'Are—are you g-going out w-with her tonight——?' The choked sensation in Jane's throat once again caused her to stammer over her words. The pain in her heart was almost physical, the anguish in her mind unbearable.

'Yes, I am.'

'Wh-where are—are you g-going?' Jane's voice held a plea, a plea for him to change his mind. She was *willing* him to change his mind.

'To the Regent,' he answered, his voice sulky now as guilt began to penetrate the cold determination with which he had embarked on his confession.

'The Regent—for dinner—and—d-dancing?'

Don gave a smothered exclamation.

'For heaven's sake, Jane, stop torturing yourself, will you! Yes, we're dancing and dining! You'll soon find someone else and do the same yourself!' He glanced at the clock. 'I'm going up to change. Why don't you go and see Nora? She's a good friend and you can confide in her. It'll do you good!' And with that he was gone, striding past her as she stood close to the door.

'Come back,' she cried beseechingly, her hands outstretched. 'Don, I love you! Don't go to this other girl! I love you and need you....' Her voice faded as he swept upstairs and closed the bedroom door. It wasn't happening, she told herself again. Don could not be so unkind; he had never been unkind to her, not really. Impatient sometimes lately, as if he were under some kind of a strain. She had believed it to be his work, and all the overtime he had been putting in. Overtime....

'It seems,' she said to him when at last he came down, spruce and handsome in the light blue lounge suit she had bought him for Christmas, along with the lowered shirt and the gold cuff-links, 'that I've failed you—physically?' She was a little calmer now, at least outwardly.

'Gina's experienced; she does attract me physically,' admitted Don, not attempting to avoid his wife's accusing gaze. 'I can't help it, Jane, it's human to err——'

'Don't!' she broke in angrily. 'What would you say if the positions were reversed—if it were I who'd been unfaithful?'

He frowned and muttered sulkily,

'Women are different from men.'

The old cry! What price equality of the sexes when a man could still say a thing like that?

'I'll move into the other bedroom,' she said dully. 'Have—have a—a—good t-time....'

It was over a week before Jane could bring herself to go and see her friend Nora Bakewell, whose husband, Roger, having recently started up on his own in the house decorating business, often worked at the week-ends. Nora was delighted when Jane rang to say she would be coming on the Sunday afternoon.

'Roger's working and I wasn't looking forward to my own company; come early and we'll have a long natter before tea.'

It was obvious that Nora had taken it for granted that Don would be with her, and Jane paused a long while before saying.

'I'll be on my own, Nora—but I can stay to tea.'

'On your own?' There was no mistaking the surprise in her friend's voice, and again Jane hesitated before speaking.

'I'll tell you all about it when I come.'

'Something wrong?' enquired Nora anxiously.

'Very wrong, but I can't talk over the phone. I'll be with you after lunch.'

It was a couple of hours later when Nora said, bewilderment and disbelief mingling with the anger in her voice,

'You mean that Don's willing to break his home up—finish, just like that!'

Jane nodded her head.

'He's very determined, Nora, so there's nothing for it but to let everything go. I couldn't live there on my own—not—n-not with all—all the m-memories.' Valiantly she held back the tears, but she was biting her lip till it hurt. 'He's madly in love with her.'

'My God! Men! What in heaven's name are they made of!'

'I'd never have believed Don could hurt me like he has. He was so callous about it all.'

'Guilty conscience, obviously, the——!' Nora managed to stop herself in time. 'What are your plans, then?'

'I can't think straight, Nora!'

'Apparently one gets over this sort of thing—eventually.'

'I suppose so.' Jane bit her lip hard to stop its trembling. Life without Don.... The loneliness, the darkness, the anguish of knowing he was with another woman. 'I feel that if I could get away temporarily I'd be able to accept the position more easily. I'd become resigned. But I'm seeing Don every morning....' Jane shuddered as the picture came before her eyes—the picture of Don sitting there, eating the breakfast she had prepared for him, his face hard, his eyes indifferent if on occasions they should happen to meet her piteously pleading ones. 'Even a fortnight might help.'

'Then why not have a holiday, right away? Josie has a caravan in Wales; I'm sure she'd let you have it for a couple of weeks.' Nora paused, then frowned, glancing out of the window to the bleak aspect of drizzle and dark grey skies. 'You'd be more miserable than ever, shut away in a caravan all by yourself. You want company, and the sun. How about a cruise?'

Already Jane was shaking her head.

'I haven't any money, Nora. We've had a big expense lately, with that repair to the roof. It took all we had.' And now, she thought bitterly, Don was spending his money on another girl.

'I'd certainly think about getting right away, but if you've no money....' Nora gave a deep sigh and for a moment it seemed she would say something grossly insulting about Don, but she thought better of it, merely asking Jane if she knew anything about the girl in whom Don had become interested.

'Her name's Gina,' said Jane briefly.

Nora stared at the dejected figure of her friend.

'I'll make a cup of tea,' she decided, 'and then we'll talk this thing over.' She was brisk suddenly, but Jane failed to see how she could offer any sort of help. She spoke as soon as Nora returned with the tea tray.

'Don says she's vivacious, and—and experienced in—in lovemaking.' Jane averted her head, embarrassed by what she had said, and wishing she had not said it at all.

'Ho! She is, is she?' The tray was put down with a little bang. 'Good for him! I hope she turns out to be a nymphomaniac!'

The tea was poured, and the two girls talked. It was a dreary, almost morbid conversation, getting them nowhere.

'I feel so helpless!' said Nora exasperatedly. 'I ought to be doing something to help you, making some sort of practical suggestions—but I can't think of anything!'

'I'm on my own in this,' said Jane, wishing her aunt were still alive so that she could go and live with her for a while. 'Don's said he'll do everything——' She spread her hands helplessly. She was drained, feeling herself to be suspended in a void where logical thought could find no place. 'I wish it were all over.'

Nora said nothing; she was beginning to think that she ought to change the subject, attempt to jerk her friend out of this terrible depression that was quite plainly bringing her close to tears. The rain had stopped; she suggested a stroll and Jane instantly agreed. They spent an hour and a half out of doors and when they returned Roger was home. He stared in surprise at Jane but, catching a look from his wife as he opened his mouth to ask where Don was, he tactfully refrained from putting the question.

'I didn't expect you home, yet, Roger.' Nora was clearly glad to see him, though. 'You said you'd be working until around eight.'

'I intended to, going on to the Davises' when I'd finished Mrs Hilditch's kitchen.'

His wife nodded, faintly puzzled.

'Yes. You said there wasn't much to do at Mrs Hilditch's.'

'That's right, but when I arrived at the Davises' they couldn't be bothered with me.'

'Couldn't——?' Nora stared at him. 'They were *expecting* you! It's their guest room you were intending to make a start on, you said?'

'They've got guests—two youngsters who are suddenly without parents. You remember my saying that the Davises had two children always running in and out of their house?——children of a Mr and Mrs Scott?'

'Yes, I remember. They were there all the time you were papering the sitting-room.'

'Their father walked out on them three weeks ago, went off abroad somewhere. It seems that this couple, who lived next door but one to the Davises, seemed very happy, but in fact they weren't. There'd been some talk of a separation for a while, and the Davises were rather troubled about it, especially Mrs Davis, because she adores those two kids.'

'Tamsin and Barry, I think you said their names are?'

'Yes, Barry's the elder by eighteen months. He's seven.'

'Why has Mrs Davis got them? Their mother——'

'She's dead.'

'*Dead!*'

'Went out—upset, I guess—and stepped under a car. Died in hospital two days later. Mrs Davis took the children and she's had them ever since.'

'How—awful!' Nora looked ready to cry. 'The poor babes! Do they know about their mother?'

'Mrs Davis seems to have put something over to them. They seemed resigned to staying with her and her husband for a while.'

'She's probably told them their mummy's ill.' Nora

paused a moment thoughtfully. 'The father—I expect the local authority's searching for him?'

Jane, standing there listening to the conversation, found her own troubles being overshadowed by the plight of those two little children. It was fortunate that they were with someone they knew, and not in a home, but all the same, they must be feeling anxious and insecure, bewildered by what was happening to them.

'They've made no headway at all,' Roger was saying in answer to his wife's question. 'It'll be difficult to find him if he's gone abroad. He's probably covered his tracks anyway, seeing that he was obviously intending to shirk all responsibility towards both his wife and his children.'

'Men!' exploded Nora with a swift glance at her friend. 'He wants shooting!'

'Will they eventually have to go into a home?' asked Jane. 'Or will the Davises take them—as foster-children, perhaps?'

Roger shook his head.

'Mrs Davis would have to give up her job. She's taking time off as it is. But she earns a very high salary and wouldn't let it go. In any case, she admitted that, much as she likes the children, she couldn't have them permanently.'

'It's good of her to have them now,' mused Jane.

'It is. She said she couldn't bear to see them taken off and put into a home. She's written to some relative of Mrs Scott who lives in Mauritius. It seems that the children's mother used to talk a lot about this Frenchman—a *blanc* Mauritian, he's called—who's a distant cousin of hers, and the only relation she'd got.

Mrs Davis asked the police to look for the address among Mrs Scott's belongings. They found it and gave it to her, and she asked permission of the local authority to write to him.'

'Has he ever met the children?' asked Jane.

'No, never.'

'Is he married?' Nora was frowning heavily. 'I don't expect his wife'll want two children she's never even seen.'

'He's a bachelor, and not a young one, either. He's thirty-five, so Mrs Scott told Mrs Davis, and he's interested only in his estate. He has sugar plantations and a modern sugar refinery. He's one of the old aristocracy whose ancestors went to the island during the times of the slave trade. They ruled like lords—some of them still do, I believe, and this man, Philippe de Chameral, is one of them.'

'It's fascinating,' commented Nora, but went on to say that this Frenchman was hardly the man to take two young children into his care. 'Apart from anything else,' added Nora thoughtfully, 'a thirty-five-year-old bachelor would be totally unsuitable as a guardian for them.'

Roger shrugged, and for a moment or two Jane withdrew her attention, as she began to think of what she knew about the island of Mauritius which in most people's minds was famous only for the dodo and its postage stamps. Having always been interested in geography, Jane knew that the island was part of the Mascarene group, that it was an island of volcanic origin lying just north of the Tropic of Capricorn and almost entirely surrounded by coral reefs. It had a lovely climate and some spectacular mountain and tropical jungle scenery, to say nothing of its numerous, unspoiled beaches. Its peoples were a bewildering mixture of Europeans, Chinese, Africans and Indians.

'If this man did take them,' Nora was saying thoughtfully, 'he'd have to employ a nanny, so it's most unlikely that he *will* offer to take them.'

But it was to transpire that Nora was wrong. Philippe de Chameral surprised everyone by his letter to Mrs Davis saying that he would be willing to give the children a home until their father was found. Jane heard all this when, after the children's plight had troubled her for more than a week, she rang her friend to ask if the father had been found yet.

'No, not a trace! But guess what? This Frenchman's agreed to take them! I was amazed, seeing that he's never even met them!'

'I'm so glad—When will they be going?'

'When someone's found to take them....' Nora's voice slowly drifted away to silence.

'Are you still there, Nora?'

'Yes—er—yes, of course....' Another silence, Jane looked at the receiver, a frown between her eyes.

'Nora—are you still there?' she repeated.

'Look, Jane, I've just had the brightest idea that's come to me in years! Come on over, love! As quickly as you can!'

'Now? But——'

'Yes, now!' The line went dead and again Jane frowned at the receiver. It was not like Nora to act so strangely as this.

An hour and a half later, having listened to Nora's 'bright idea', Jane was on the bus, on her way to see

Mrs Davis, Nora having arranged the interview immediately she had Jane's assurance that she would be willing to take the children to their 'uncle' in Mauritius.

Jane had listened with ever increasing interest as Nora told her that Philippe de Chameral had asked Mrs Davis to find a trustworthy lady to bring the two children out to him. He would send the first-class fares and money for incidental expenses. The lady would be given a fortnight's holiday in a first-class hotel, plus a sum of money in payment for her service in bringing the children safely into his care.

'It sounds wonderful.' Jane, although still very much weighed down by misery and despair at the forthcoming break-up of her marriage, was at the same time profoundly conscious of her good fortune in having an opportunity like this come to her at the very time she needed to get away from her husband and her home. Of course, there was the hurdle of Mrs Davis's approval to get over but, listening to her friend on the telephone as she arranged the appointment, Jane could not help but be optimistic about the effect which Nora's recommendation would have on Mrs Davis.

'What a relief that it's all been fixed up so simply,' Mrs Davis was saying less than half an hour after Jane had arrived at her house. 'I'd a horror of advertising for someone because I felt sure I'd be inundated with applicants who were more interested in the money and the holiday than in the children themselves. They're upset at the change that's taken place in their lives. I've had to tell Barry that his mother's dead, but of course I didn't say how she met her death. The whole thing's so tragic, and I can only hope and pray that this uncle will treat the poor little mites kindly.'

'I should think he will, seeing that he's so willing to have them,' returned Jane reasonably.

'Yes, I'm sure you're right, Mrs Clark. It's really a miracle that he has agreed to have them, for I'm sure he's one of those men who's very content with his peaceful bachelor way of life. That is certainly the impression I had from poor Mrs Scott—although she did admit that she had not seen the man for over ten years.'

'What was the relationship?' enquired Jane interestedly.

'Mrs Scott's sister married a cousin of this man. But as Mrs Scott's sister is dead and this cousin too, it seems more incredible than ever that Monsieur de Chameral will have them, for I'm sure he's really no relation at all.'

'No. . . .' Jane had to agree, and she herself was set wondering about the Frenchman's generosity in being so ready to take on the role of guardian to the children. And it transpired that there were no snags to contend with. The fares were forwarded as soon as Mrs Davis cabled to say that a suitable young lady had been found to bring the children over to him.

'I'd rather be known as Miss Clark,' Jane had said to Nora when, the same evening, she was again with her friend, as Roger was away, working late. 'I don't quite know why, but I feel that this man might ask me awkward questions if he knows I'm married because, after all, not many wives would want to leave their husbands at home while they took a holiday of this kind, would they?'

'No, I agree, I'll ring Mrs Davis and tell her to give

your name as Miss Clark. I'd better do it now because she'll probably be sending Philippe de Chameral a cable first thing in the morning.' Nora looked at her friend. 'It seems like fate that this has come up just at this particular time, when we were saying that what you needed was to get right away.'

Jane merely nodded; a moment later she was left on her own as Nora went to telephone Mrs Davis. What explanation would Nora give? Jane wondered. It didn't matter anyway. Her mind reverted to what Nora had said about fate. Yes, it was a strange unfathomable thing, for if Roger hadn't started up on his own he'd never have met Mrs Davis, and the children. And if she, Jane, had not had Nora for a friend.... So many 'ifs', but that seemed to be what fate was all about—nothing really tangible or concrete. Well, at least she had an object in life now, even though it was a very temporary one. Into the dark abyss of her misery a light had appeared; it provided the diversion she so badly needed to take her mind off her own troubles.

The great jumbo jet made a smooth landing at Plaisance Airport and Jane and her charges were soon going through Customs. The flight on the whole had been enjoyable, though Jane soon concluded that travelling first-class had a lot to do with it, since the long flight would have been boring for the children if she had not had the facilities for bringing out the games and puzzles and colouring books which she had had the foresight to bring with her. The children had slept for a while and then, as the flight neared its end, they had all disembarked at Nairobi, where a stop of over an hour was made. So all in all it had not been too

tedious for the children. True, Tamsin had become
fractious on occasions at the inactivity, but Jane had
successfully managed to coax her out of her ill-humour.

They were met by an Indo-Mauritian who, spotting
them immediately they had been cleared by Customs,
introduced himself as Bhoosan, Monsieur de Chameral's chauffeur. He spoke in perfect English, which
was the official language of the island, although the
native language of Europeans and educated Creoles was
French. The Indians spoke Hindi; the Chinese also
spoke their own language.

'We have a long ride, I'm afraid,' Bhoosan informed
Jane, his glance flickering to the children. 'I expect
the little ones are tired already?'

'They slept for a time but, yes, they are rather tired.'

'Monsieur de Chameral told you of the fairly long
drive to his home?'

'Yes, he did—at least, he told the lady who had
charge of the children.' Bhoosan was seeing them into
the car so Jane got into the back seat without waiting
for him to come round to where she was standing. Barry
wanted to move, so that he could be near her. She
smiled, and slid an arm around each child, marvelling
that in such a short space of time they could have en-
deared themselves to her so strongly. Tamsin was a
darling. Silver-haired and with baby blue eyes, she
was like a little doll, while her brother, a sturdy seven-
year-old with the same blue eyes but hair of a lightish
brown, possessed the sort of confidence that astounded
Jane. She had never had much to do with children,
but she felt sure that Barry was far more confident and
intelligent than most children of his age. To her relief
they had not spoken of their parents at all on the flight,

but they did talk a great deal about this uncle they were going to live with, wanting to know what his house was like, and if the sun really did shine all the time on his island, just as Mrs Davis said it did.

Once the car had left the airport the children began to take a keen interest in what was rolling by along the road and, left to her own thoughts, Jane reflected for a space on the letter she had received, via Mrs Davis, from the children's uncle. Written in a clear, authoritative hand, it gave concise and definite instructions with not one superfluous word, even the ending being stiff and formal;

'Yours truly,
Philippe de Chameral.'

'Discouraging,' Mrs Davis had declared, with an anxious glance at the children. 'I'm not altogether happy, but what else could we have done? The local authority wouldn't have wasted much time before taking the mites into care.'

'I feel sure that they'll be far happier with their uncle than in care, Mrs Davis,' said Jane in an attempt to reassure her.

Mrs Davis nodded, said something about foreigners being unpredictable and then lapsed into silence as she again perused the letter which Jane had given her to read.

Well, mused Jane as the car sped along at a modest speed, following the coast as far as Belle Mare before veering inland, taking a north-western direction to Grand Bay, where the Chateau de Chameral was situated, she would soon be meeting this Frenchman and assessing his worth as a guardian to Barry and Tamsin.

'Look, Miss Clark!' Barry was pointing to a white-domed Indian temple on the roadside. 'What is it?'

Bhoosan answered, as he had been answering questions for the past few minutes, his infinite patience a sure indication that he had children of his own.

'I thought they'd be so tired that they would not have much interest in looking out of the window.' Bhoosan spoke over his shoulder as he negotiated a dangerous bend.

'They've wakened up, obviously.'

'Look——' The exclamation came from Tamsin this time, as a small mongoose crossed the road, moving leisurely so that the children had a good view of its dark, furry body.

'There are many flowers in Mauritius,' said Bhoosan after a small silence. 'The climate's very excellent for growing things.'

The children were exclaiming again as the roadside gardens provided a glowing spectacle of colour. Bhoosan named the flowers for them—canna lilies in brilliant red, or yellow or orange; a morning glory bush, a flame vine smothering a trellis. Brilliant crimson poinsettias fringed a vast sugar plantation, while a delightful smaller version of the flower grew in wild profusion on an expanse of rough ground on the opposite side of the road. Everywhere massive volcanic boulders littered the fields, spewn out in far distant times when the volcanoes of Mauritius were active. Where the fields were cultivated these giant-sized chunks of basalt had been gathered together to form high ridges running across the land.

Jane leant back in her seat and gave a little sigh of contentment. When she embarked on this venture she had decided to thrust her troubles to the back of her mind, as this was the only way in which the break would be of benefit to her. There would be plenty of time to dwell on her problems when she got back to England. For the next fortnight she was determined to occupy her thoughts with her holiday, acutely aware that she would never again be fortunate enough to visit this part of the world.

'Oh ... what are *they* doing?' Tamsin twisted her head as the car passed a group of native women balancing heavy bundles on their heads.

Bhoosan laughed, and explained that here you often saw women carrying things on their heads.

'I'm going to try that,' decided Barry.

'You'd let it fall off,' asserted his sister.

'Why don't they let it fall off?'

'They practise a very long time,' explained Bhoosan. 'At first they do have difficulty in balancing things on their heads.'

'Do they start when they're little?' Tamsin wanted to know.

'Yes—when they're about your age, Tamsin.'

'Ooh! I'll have a try, then!'

Jane left them to Bhoosan, who seemed happy to answer all their eager questions, or merely to listen to their chatter, laughing now and then while all the time giving his expert attention to the road along which they were travelling.

Short though her acquaintance with them had been, Jane had become so fond of the children that their fate was causing her some anxiety. Despite the reassurances she had produced for Mrs Davis, she was finding herself troubled about the children's life with this cultured, aristocratic Frenchman, Philippe de Chameral. Had he considered long enough, and seriously enough, before making his decision? Was he prepared for a major change in the established way of life which, apparently, had satisfied him up till now? Had he arranged for someone to look after the children—a nanny or a governess? These and other disturbing questions flitted through Jane's mind as the big, luxurious car bowled along, through varied scenery of sugar plantations, or wilder terrain, then on to a region where the cultivation of tea predominated. There were narrow winding lanes and broader well-made roads; there were mimosas in the hedgerows and pinewoods in the valley. Palms became a predominant feature of the landscape, with here and there a lovely royal poinciana or a tulip tree. And all the time the distance between Jane and her destination was being reduced.

CHAPTER TWO

AT last the car swung off the road and swept through beautiful white gates to travel along an avenue of coquetuche trees beneath which flourished a breathtaking array of canna lilies, allamandas, and spray orchids. At the end of the avenue stood a magnificent white house ... the Chateau de Chameral....

It was a turreted, porticoed colonial mansion in a resplendent setting of unique beauty, the multicoloured grounds abounding with jacarandas, oleanders, hibiscus and bougainvillaea. Long terraces formed a distinctive feature; there were smooth green lawns and a pond of giant water-lilies. A gorgeous swimming-pool could be seen through an ornamental arch, and there was the subtle awareness of little hidden arbours shaded by tropical trees and bushes. To one side of the extensive grounds was a tract of the island's natural, untamed jungle vegetation, while to the north was a vista of casuarinas with the translucent blue of the Indian Ocean no more than a step away, its waters— the warmest in the world—caressing a beach of pure silver sand. The lagoon, sleepy and enticing, changed colour with the rise and fall of the sun, Bhoosan had told Jane, and even now, as they got out of the car, the sun was setting in the west, its fire painting the tranquil waters and the tip of the coral reef beyond.

'Is this it?' Tamsin murmured in an awed voice.

'Yes, dear, this is your uncle's house.' Jane had been

prepared for something out of the ordinary, but never had she pictured splendour such as this. Like something out of a fairy-tale, it was delightfully entrancing but unreal.

There was nothing unreal, however, about the welcoming smile of Silva, Monsieur de Chameral's butler, as he opened the door seconds after Bhoosan had rung the bell. Silva spoke to Bhoosan in French, then stood aside and said,

'Come in, mademoiselle. Monseigneur is waiting— This way, please.' He swept a hand towards a door at the far end of the hall. Jane noticed that Bhoosan was attending to the children's luggage. She reminded him to leave hers in the car, as she would be leaving almost at once.

The hall, air-conditioned, with cool white walls, was both simple and tasteful in its decor, its chief feature being the tall-growing plants whose branches adorned the massive arches before rising to the ceiling. Barry ventured bravely behind the butler, but Tamsin, still overawed by the sheer magnificence and size of the house, sought urgently for Jane's hand and clung to it with a sort of frightened desperation.

Silva knocked quietly and opened the door. Jane entered, holding Tamsin's hand, and with the other urging Barry forward, into the room. She heard the door close behind Silva, felt Tamsin's small fingers tighten round her own.

The room was large and high, with a massive desk by the window and numerous filing cabinets along one wall. Jane took a fleeting glance around as the man rose from the desk at which he had been sitting. She was immediately struck by his superior height, his lean good looks, his unmistakable air of breeding. He came forward, a hand outstretched, Jane extended her own and felt the firmness of his grasp, her eyes moving from his crisp mid-brown hair to the high forehead, faintly lined above straight dark eyebrows. His lazy, slate-grey eyes were arresting, but no more so than his firm, enigmatic mouth and jutting chin. His skin was tight, clear, with the colour and sheen of an antique bronze.

The hand extended was the same colour, deceptively slender, with long, sensitive fingers.

'Good afternoon, Miss Clark. I'm happy to meet you.'

'Good afternoon, Monseigneur....' Jane's voice trailed uncertainly. She wondered if this was the way she should be addressing him.

'I hope the long flight was not too tedious for you?' His glance went fleetingly to the children before returning to Jane.

'It was most enjoyable,' she returned shyly. 'The children were a little restless now and then, but on the whole they were quite happy. I'd brought some games and puzzles to occupy them.'

'That was thoughtful of you.' His manner was courteous but cool and detached. 'So these are my cousin's two children. How do you do, Barry?' A hand was offered and Barry took it reluctantly. Watching his expression, Jane saw at once that the child was not at all impressed with this uncle with whom he was to make his home. 'And you're Tamsin.' Monsieur de Chameral looked down at her in silence for a moment. 'You're five, I'm told?'

'Five and—and a h-half,' she stammered nervously.

Jane looked at their uncle, anxiety in her eyes.

'I hope they'll settle,' she said. 'All this has been a terrible upheaval for them.'

'Undoubtedly. They're young, though, and therefore resilient. Children, like animals, are not long troubled by memories.'

Jane looked at him sharply. He sounded so indifferent, lacking in understanding of what the children must be going through. Tamsin was staring at the man; she moved a little closer to Jane, who felt the trembling of the small body against her.

'Have you a nanny for them?' asked Jane, feeling it was a liberty to question the man but forced by her anxiety to do so.

'She'll be here a week tomorrow,' he told her. 'Did you get my letter explaining that I hadn't been able to get someone to come right away, and that I'd like you to stay for these eight days and look after the children?'

Already Jane was shaking her head.

'No, the letter hadn't arrived when I left home.'

'I did wonder if I was in time. I couldn't let you know sooner because this lady didn't let *me* know. It was at first agreed that she would be here when you arrived.' He looked down at Jane from his great height and said, 'If you stay, Miss Clark, I'll make it worth your while. You'll still have the full fortnight's holiday at the St Geran Hotel if you have the time. If not, you'll have only a week—but as I've said, I shall make it worth your while.'

Barry, who had been listening to this, moved close to Jane and pushed his hand into hers.

'Please stay with us, Miss Clark,' he begged. 'I want

you to stay.' His big eyes were moist, but he was bravely holding back the tears.

'I want you to stay as well,' faltered Tamsin, also on the verge of tears. 'I'm—I'm frightened.'

'Frightened?' repeated her uncle, frowning. 'What is there to be frightened of?'

So stiff! thought Jane, more than ever nonplussed by his agreeing to take the children.

'You....' quivered Tamsin, turning her face into Jane's skirt. 'I w-want to g-go home to my mummy and—and daddy!' she cried in a muffled voice.

Jane and Monsieur de Chameral glanced at one another. She wondered if he had any heart at all, for there was no apparent softening of his expression.

'Will you stay?' he asked again. She answered without hesitation, the holiday becoming totally unimportant.

'Yes, I'll be glad to stay, Monseigneur.'

'Thank you, Miss Clark.' His cool and distant manner remained as he went on to say that he had already had a room prepared hoping she would agree to stay. He then got down to the business of her payment, appearing to be faintly amused at her embarrassment as he told her what he would give her for the eight days she would be with him. He spoke in a clipped abrupt voice, never using two words where one would do. Jane learned that the hotel he had chosen for her was opened only two years ago, and that it was one of the most select hotels in Mauritius. She was looking forward to going there but at the same time she was acutely conscious of the fact that if she met the children's nanny, and did not like her, then the holiday would certainly not give her the pleasure which she had anticipated on first leaving home.

'And now,' said Monsieur de Chameral finally, 'I'll
ring for Meri, who will take you to your rooms.' His
glance fell to Barry, and Jane wondered if she imagined
it or had the suspicion of a smile touched his lips
momentarily?

The maid, a slender, dark-eyed Creole, took them
upstairs and along an arched corridor to a suite of
rooms at the far end.

'Would you like me to unpack for you?' she asked,
glancing at the four suitcases that had already been
brought up.

'Later, if you don't mind,' replied Jane. She wanted
to have a few minutes alone with the children, hoping to soothe away their fears and uncertainty. 'My
two suitcases are still in the car.'

'I'll ask Bhoosan to bring them up for you, mademoiselle.'

'Thank you.'

Meri went out, closing the door softly behind her.

'I don't l-like it here,' began Tamsin tearfully, her
big baby eyes trying to take it all in as she looked
around her. 'Can we go home, Miss Clark?'

'We can't go to Mummy and Daddy,' said her
brother. 'Mummy's not there and Daddy's lost.' His
face puckered and two big tears rolled down his pale,
plump little cheeks.

'I'm staying with you for a little while,' said Jane,
herself on the point of tears. 'Come and see what's
outside.' She took their hands and led them to the
balcony. Dusk was short and it would be dark by half-
past six. But there was still sufficient light to see the
gardens and the sandy shore and the beautiful lagoon,

sleepy and still, in the gathering, purple-tinted twilight. 'Tomorrow we'll go on the sands and build a great big castle. How will you like that?'

'I want to go home,' fretted Tamsin.

'Will you stay with us all the time, Miss Clark?'

'I can't, Barry darling. I've just said that I'll stay a little while.'

'Where will you go after that?' he wanted to know.

'I'm having a holiday and then I'm going home, back to England.'

'To your mummy?'

'No, dear, not to my mummy.' Jane pointed to some sea birds swooping and diving by the edge of the reef. She was hoping to divert the children and to her relief she succeeded.

After a short time it was too dark to see anything and they came back into the room. It was a beautifully furnished bedroom with a bathroom off. Another door led to a sitting-room and off from that was another bedroom in which were two single beds. So Philippe de Chameral had put the children together, a circumstance for which Jane was exceedingly thankful, as she strongly suspected that neither would have settled had they been put in separate bedrooms.

They were tired but no longer tearful, and Jane decided to ask for their meal to be brought up to the sitting-room and she would put them to bed immediately after it.

There was a bell and she rang it, Meri came without delay and nodded smilingly when Jane told her what she wanted.

'I will have Cook see to it, mademoiselle, at once.'

Two hours later Jane was reading in the sitting-room when she received the message that Monseigneur was waiting for her in the dining saloon.

'Oh!' she blinked. 'Er—I didn't know I was expected to join him for dinner.'

'Yes, miss,' said Rima, the Indo-Mauritian girl who had brought the message. 'He told me to lay an extra cover.'

Disconcerted, Jane fumbled for some feasible excuse for not going down, but none came.

'I'll be as quick as I can,' she said. 'Please tell Monseigneur that I'm sorry to keep him waiting——'

'I think he understands, miss. He did say he forgot to tell you that you'd be dining with him this evening.'

Jane nodded, watched the girl leave and then hurriedly went to the bathroom to take a shower.

She appeared in the dining saloon less than twenty minutes later, looking extremely young and pretty in a two-piece of deep red cotton. The skirt, gathered into a wide waistband, was very full with heavy silk embroidery at the bottom; the top was tight-fitting, with a low-cut neckline and three-quarter puff sleeves. It was a 'gypsy' style, and suited Jane's dark hair to perfection. She wore loop earrings, and a thin gold bangle, both of which matched the style of the two-piece.

They looked at one another as she entered, Philippe de Chameral's expression enigmatic as his lazy grey eyes slid over Jane's slender figure before settling for a moment on her face. Jane herself felt almost mesmerised by the image of masculine perfection confronting her. The man was standing with his back to an enormous window looking out on to a courtyard shaped by royal palms and with coloured lamps effectively concealed in the bushes, and again she was struck by his clear-cut, handsome features, by his air of distinction and good breeding. His skin seemed darker than before, contrasting as it did with the whiteness of his dinner jacket and shirt.

Jane advanced slowly from the door, conscious of his penetrating eyes flickering over her for the second time, conscious of her colour fluctuating, of the nervousness within her at being in the presence of someone so much above her.

'I'm sorry I'm late,' she began, when he raised a hand, palm towards her.

'That was not your fault, mademoiselle. I apologise for my omission in not informing you that you'd be dining here, with me, while you are my guest.'

'I rather regard myself as your employee, Monseigneur,' returned Jane, deciding to follow the formal manner he was adopting.

'You have obliged me by staying, and I regard you as my guest.' He pulled out a chair for her and she sat down, her appreciative glance sweeping over the table and its contents. The table itself was old, with a patina that revealed innumerable hours of hard work on the part of servants. The table mats and coasters were of silver; the cutlery too, and exquisitely engraved with the owner's monogram on the handle of each piece. There were flowers and candles and beautifully embroidered serviettes. Jane had rarely know such luxury, her visits to expensive hotels having been limited to birthdays and anniversaries. She wondered if the Frenchman always dined like this, or had some of it been put on for her benefit? She decided it had not.

Each course was superb, washed down with a wine that went to her head just sufficiently to make her forget everything but the present moment—the handsome, cultured Frenchman who, she had already grasped, was like some feudal overlord, ruling over his vast sugar estate—the elegantly laid out table, the delicious food, the soft music which came from four speakers, one in each corner of the room. Again she experienced that sensation of unreality; she was filled with wonderment that she should be here at all, in this luxurious mansion, dining with its noble owner, Philippe de Chameral.

'I expect you work for a living, Miss Clark,' he had said when they were seated at the table, their wineglasses filled, and the first course being served. 'Were you on holiday? Was that the reason you could bring the children over at this particular time?'

Jane had paused, reluctant to lie, but at the same time unwilling to go into details as to the real reason why she was able to accept the mission.

'Yes, Monseigneur,' she said resignedly at length. 'I happened to—to have some free time.' She had taken up her knife and fork and cut herself a piece of smoked salmon. She avoided his keen, alert gaze . . . and felt instinctively that he knew her action was deliberate.

'Tell me about the children,' he invited later. 'You don't know very much, of that I'm fully aware.'

She explained that a friend of hers had been the go-between, and that Mrs Davis had welcomed her offer as she was troubled about the result had she been forced to advertise for someone.

Philippe de Chameral was nodding slowly.

'It would have been a gamble. Yes, it was a most fortunate circumstance that you were able to bring them to me.' He paused a moment, then added, 'I'm sorry about your holiday not starting right away. I've been in touch with the manager of the hotel and explained. I hope you are not too disappointed?'

Jane shook her head at once.

'Not in the least,' she replied. 'I want to stay with them. They're very lost at present, Monsieur de Chameral. And insecure. Children flounder when their lives are upset in this way. First it was their father whom they missed, then their mother, and now they are brought here, to a strange house in a strange country, and——' She broke off, looking at him.

'And a strange man for their guardian,' he finished for her.

Jane nodded.

'So you can perhaps imagine how dreadfully lost they're feeling? That's why I'm so willing to stay with them until their nanny arrives.'

'Very satisfactory. They seem to like you, Miss Clark.'

'We all took to one another,' she smiled. 'It was fortunate.'

'Very fortunate.' He took up the wine bottle and topped up her glass, then his own. 'Meri will of course do certain things for them. She's a Creole and they might feel strange with her at first, but they'll soon get used to her. She has a particularly charming way with children, I've noticed.'

His words about the children becoming used to Meri was to prove correct; within two days Barry was telling Jane that he liked Meri, who had promised to give him

some pretty seashells which she had picked up on th
beach.

Tamsin was taking longer. All the first day she wa
silent, having turned in on herself. She merely watched
when Jane and Barry made a castle on the beach
ignoring Jane's invitation to join in the fun. The fol
lowing day she was a little better, though Jane coul
not coax a smile out of her, much less a laugh. By th
third day she was definitely coming round; she played
quite happily at hide-go-seek with her brother in th
grounds of the chateau while Jane, clad in shorts and
a brief top, took the sun and kept a watchful eye on
her charges at the same time.

'Are you getting used to it now?' she ventured
when, having tired themselves out, the children cam
to her, breathless, and flopped down on the grass by
her chair. Jane was looking at Tamsin when she asked
the question, but it was Barry who answered.

'I like the sunshine, and I like the sands to play
on. But I don't like Uncle Philippe. He doesn't tal
to us like Daddy did, or play with us in the garden.'

'He hasn't much time, Barry dear. You see, he ha
lots and lots of fields which grow sugar—I showed you
the big canes where the sugar comes from, remember?

'Yes.' Barry's face puckered a little. 'It doesn't look
like sugar, what's in there.'

'Well, it is, but never mind that just now. I wa
saying that Uncle Philippe hasn't much time to play
with you, because he has lots and lots of work to do.

'I like the sunshine.' Tamsin spoke at last, her face
far less strained than it had been for the first two days
'But I wish you were staying with us, Miss Clark. I
don't like that other lady what's coming to mind us.'

'You haven't seen her yet,' Jane said with a lightness she was far from feeling. In such a short time she had grown to love the children, and to leave them would undoubtedly be a wrench. But it was not her own feelings which occupied her mind. She was more concerned about the children than ever, and knew now that it would have been far better if she had delivered them and then gone out of their lives at once. As it was, they had grown used to her; they had taken to her, relying on her, trusting her. She had infinite patience and understanding; it was no hardship to play with them like this, to read them bedtime stories. She would have liked to take them a little further afield, but her employer had not offered her the use of the car and so her journeyings with the children had consisted of walks along the shore and the lanes, and rambles in the grounds of the chateau itself.

'Why can't you stay with us always, Miss Clark?' Barry asked the question later that day when Jane had taken him and Tamsin on to the sands and they were building a castle. 'We want you to stay with us, don't we, Tamsin?'

'Yes, for ever and ever!'

'It isn't possible, darlings.' Jane's manner was gentle, her mind on her home and the husband who neither loved nor wanted her. Here, she was both loved and wanted.'

'Don't you like it? Is that why you won't stay with us?' Barry's fingers were busy with some brightly-coloured flags which he was placing on the castle walls.

'No, that isn't the reason, Barry. Your uncle wouldn't want me. He's already got this other nice lady coming to look after you.'

'She isn't as nice as you,' said Barry stoutly. 'Nobody could be as nice as you!'

'Of course she's nice. Your uncle wouldn't have engaged her if she wasn't nice.'

'What does engaged mean?'

'It means that your uncle is having her to work here, at the chateau, as your nanny. Do you know what a nanny is?'

'Yes,' said Tamsin. 'A little girl in my story book has a nanny. She's nice and she laughs and has curly hair.'

'I don't want a nanny.' Barry was speaking softly, as if to himself, as he continued to stick in the flags, taking some out and putting others in their place. 'I only want you. . . .'

Jane bit her lip, half wishing she had not come here to Mauritius at all. However, the children soon recovered their spirits, and for the next couple of days nothing was mentioned about their new nanny.

Apart from the time she spent with him at dinner each evening Jane saw little of the noble owner of the chateau; he seemed either to be in his study or over at the refinery where he had a private office in the main block. Meri, expansive in the nicest way, often dropped pieces of information to Jane and in this way she had learned a little about his habits. She also heard about the English girl, Yvette Sutcliffe who, it was rumoured, would eventually become the wife of Philippe and mistress of his home. Jane was surprised, wondering how this young lady would take to the children.

'Miss Sutcliffe's father's an investor who came over

ere to start a factory making electrical equipment,'
Meri said in answer to Jane's tentative enquiry as to
now this Yvette came to be living on the island. 'Mr
Sutcliffe came several years ago and his wife and
daughter followed a year later. Miss Sutcliffe's twenty-
eight and very beautiful.' A smile spread over Meri's
pretty face. 'She is very suitable for Monseigneur, as
he too is very handsome, don't you think?'

Jane nodded and said unhesitatingly,

'Yes, very handsome indeed.' She was curious about
this girl whom Meri had mentioned, because her impression of Philippe de Chameral was that he was a
confirmed bachelor, set in his ways, and not inclined
to change them. However, the fact that he had agreed
to have the children indicated that he was not set
firmly against a change in his way of life. Jane thought
that if Yvette was a motherly, understanding woman
then Barry and Tamsin might well be fortunate.

'I am engaged myself,' Meri said shyly. 'His name is
Takai and he's the friend of my brother.'

'Are you getting married soon?' Jane asked, politely
showing interest.

'No, we have to save up first.'

'Where will you live?'

'We want to have a flat in Port Louis, Takai works
there, in a shop.'

'That's the capital, isn't it?'

'Yes, and it's the main port as well. There are
some good shops in Port Louis, but at Curepipe as
well.'

On another occasion Meri became expansive about
the Chateau de Chameral, telling Jane that it was a
very fine example of colonial architecture.

'It is a very graceful house, don't you think?'

'Yes, indeed,' answered Jane enthusiastically. 'I've been exploring, and everything about it delights me.' Her glance strayed to the imposing entrance and to the date carved over the door: 1782, with the fleur-de-lis above it.

'The gardens were completely French at one time, of course. But the many lakes and lovely ornamental ponds had to be destroyed because, in those days, malaria was a very great risk.'

Jane looked around, not at all sure that the lakes and ponds had been more beautiful than the lawns and terraces and exotic borders that had replaced them. She had glanced through various windows, most of which opened out on to verandahs. All the rooms had an atmosphere of elegance about them, and the furnishings and priceless antiques had left her spellbound with admiration. She thought of her own modest little home ... and wondered what her husband was doing at this moment. She had thought about him on that first evening, when she had sat down to dine with the children's uncle. Luxurious eating for her had been confined to those occasions when, for birthdays and anniversaries, she and Don would go to an expensive hotel to celebrate. Now he was taking Gina out to even more expensive hotels—and almost as an everyday occurrence. This he had admitted, saying that Gina's father was well-off and therefore she was used to dining out at the best places. Jane would not have been human if she had not wished that Don could know that she, too, was dining and wining in luxury.

More and more she found she could dismiss Don from her thoughts. It was not that her love was dying—

as she felt now she was certain it never would die—
but she seemed to have accepted the futility of allowing him to intrude into her mind. There was so much
that was new here, so many diversions, not least of
which was the children who, under her tender care,
were adapting to their new environment far quicker
than Jane would ever have believed possible. What
troubled her now was that once again they were to
suffer another mental upheaval, this time having
another stranger come to take charge of them.

The morning of the nanny's arrival dawned and
although Jane awoke to the sun pouring into her bedroom, she was conscious of an empty feeling in the
pit of her stomach. Today she was handing the children
over to their nanny. . . .

She ought to have slipped away, she thought, wishing this idea had occurred to her before, so that she
could have put it to the children's uncle. The good-
byes were going to be heartbreaking, for she feared it
would not only be the children who would shed tears.
Yes, callous as it seemed, it would have been far better
for her to have slipped away, perhaps while the children
were still in bed, leaving Meri to see to them until the
arrival of the nanny, some time during the morning.

CHAPTER THREE

THE woman arrived at the chateau at eleven o'clock, and immediately Jane saw her her heart sank. About forty-five years of age, Miss Renshawe had stern set features and a thin, straight mouth. Her blue eyes were hard and cold, her forehead lined, deeply, as if she frowned often. She was English and had recently worked for a family who were moving to the Far East, a part of the world which Miss Renshawe disliked and therefore was unwilling to go there. How Philippe de Chameral had come to hear of her Jane did not know, nor was she interested. She was filled with misgivings, deeply troubled by the idea of two sensitive young children being put into the care of a person who, Jane felt sure, would not even try to understand what they were going through.

Philippe de Chameral made the introductions, having already had Jane in his study, to thank her and to give her the fee for her services. Bhoosan would be at liberty to take her to the hotel, he had said. He hoped she would enjoy her stay.

The children were sent for a few minutes after Miss Renshawe arrived; they were brought in by Meri and presented to their nanny. Tamsin's face changed instantly, and a frozen expression came over it. Jane felt a lump in her throat as the child's small hand came up and clutched hers, as if for support. Barry's face was set, his mouth tight; it was not difficult to see that he was trying to be brave, fighting back the tears.

'Well,' began the woman briskly, 'you're Barry, are you? My name's Miss Renshawe and I'm going to look after you from now on.' The woman's voice was gruff, almost like a man's. She was big-boned, tall and overpowering even to Jane. 'Tamsin, eh? How old are you, Tamsin?'

Their uncle had remained silent, but now he spoke, saying quietly,

'I did tell you their ages, Miss Renshawe. Tamsin is five and a half and Barry seven.'

'Ah, yes! They'll be going to school, I take it?'

'Of course. My chauffeur will take them and bring them back each day. I did explain all this to you,' said Philippe de Chameral with a frown.

'I don't—w-want that lady minding m-me, I want Miss Clark....' Tamsin's small, piquant little face puckered and Jane again felt a lump in her throat, a painful constriction that brought the tears to the backs of her eyes. Tamsin was crying softly, while Barry, feeling protective, moved towards her and put his arms around her. Never had Jane witnessed such a heart-breaking scene; she knew she would remember it for the rest of her life. There was tension in the room, with Philippe de Chameral standing there looking stern, and faintly bored, and Miss Renshawe glinting down at the children, clinging to one another and both crying now, while Jane, her own eyes misty and her lips quivering, just stared dumbly in front of her, seeing nothing, but feeling her own tragedy was nothing compared to this.

'You will get used to Miss Renshawe,' their uncle said at last. 'Miss Clark, if you can stay for another hour or so, while Miss Renshawe gets settled in. . . ?'

'Of course I'll stay,' returned Jane, so promptly and eagerly that she drew Miss Renshawe's attention at once. She was subjected to an up-and-down examination, the kind that could not fail to arouse her anger. The woman must seem a veritable ogre to these two little children, decided Jane, wishing with all her heart that the Frenchman had found some understanding woman to engage a nanny for his niece and nephew instead of doing it himself.

Jane expected trouble from the children and she got it. Once away from their uncle and the woman he had engaged to care for them, they clung desperately to her and, sobbing piteously, pleaded with her not to leave them. And at last she decided to tell their uncle that she was willing to give up the idea of the holiday and stay with the children for another week, to let them get used to the change.

He was agreeable, but the nanny was not.

'It's absurd!' she told Jane when she got her on her own for a moment. 'It's very plain, Miss Clark, that you've spoiled them—even in the short time you've had them. I anticipate trouble because of it! But I've not been with children for twenty years without learning how to deal effectively with tantrums!'

Jane stood on the patio of her room, watching some children playing on the sands. She had been at the hotel for over a week, and not a day had dawned but she had awakened with a sickening feeling in the pit of her stomach at the thought of those two little children being in the care of so unsuitable a woman. She told herself over and over again that Miss Renshawe, with her long years of experience with children, must know how to treat them, but always there intruded the harshness of the woman's face and voice, the cold sternness of her attitude even in the presence of their uncle.

Jane turned at last, and went back into her room. It was delightfully furnished, mainly with bamboo. There was a luxurious bathroom off, and a window running the full length of one wall. It was on the ground floor, had its own private patio leading on to a smooth green lawn which swept down to a sandy beach lapped by the gentle waters of the lagoon. The hotel's architecture had a deliberate simplicity about it designed to incorporate in every way the beauty of the natural scenery, the gardens and beaches, the surrounding lagoons. To Jane it had everything, and her only regret was that, with so much on her mind, she was unable to enjoy to the full all that the hotel offered. She often strolled along the beach, looking at other people, listening to their laughter ... and envying them the gaiety and lightheartedness which enabled them to derive the last measure of enjoyment from their holiday.

Jane took some of the trips arranged by the management, going to Port Louis one day and admiring the lovely French colonial buildings which were situated off the palm-lined Place d'Armes, which was the main square of the city. Another day she went to Curepipe, and another to the Terres de Couleurs where weathering had caused the earth to take on several varying colours, all within a very limited area. Some of the

earth was red, some yellow, some blue or green. Close
by was a spectacular waterfall which emerged from the
primeval rocks of the island.

In the main, though, she stayed around the hotel,
where she had the choice of relaxing on her patio, on
the lawn or the beach. Meals were always taken in the
Terrace Restaurant which overlooked the swimming-
pool and the dance floor. Jane had her table reserved,
right at the front and where she had a perfect view
of the band. She had spoken to several people and at
meal times she never felt lonely, as the people at
nearby tables were friendly and throughout the meal
they would throw a few words over now and then and
Jane would answer.

It was on the last evening of her stay that Jane came
into her room to find a note lying on the dressing-table.
Puzzled, she picked it up, slitting the envelope and
withdrawing the single sheet of paper.

'I am dining at the St Geran this evening,' she read,
'and would be happy if you would join me.

Yours sincerely,

Philippe de Chameral.'

Puzzled she scanned the note again, as if searching
for a clue to what it was all about. She could not accept
that the owner of the Chateau de Chameral merely
wanted the pleasure of her company. And the only
thing she could think of was that Monsieur de Chameral, deciding to dine out for a change, and having
picked on the St Geran as a natural choice, had decided
that it would look churlish if he were not to ask her
to join him.

She dressed with extra care, glad that she had had
her hair washed and set that afternoon in readiness for

her journey home the following day. She wore a tur-
quoise blue evening gown trimmed with silver ribbon;
it was sleek yet very feminine, with a cape-like feature
which was for ornament only, thrown away from her
shoulders to fall in gentle folds from the back of the
neck to the waistline. She stood for a long while regarding herself in the mirror, thinking of the first—and
only—time she had worn this dress. Don had treated
her to it, a wedding anniversary present which she
had worn that evening when her husband took her to
a hotel for dinner and dancing.

Strange that she felt no pull of sentiment or regret.
It was as if, since coming here to Mauritius, she had
become immune to her own hurt, perhaps because of
the deep anxiety she was feeling about the children.

The head waiter conducted her to another table,
but one as well placed as her own. Philippe de Chameral was already there; he rose on seeing her and the
merest trace of a smile touched the enigmatic outline
of his mouth. He was in a suit of off-white elegance
with a draped line of casual informality. His tie bore
a heraldic design just below the knot.

'Good evening, Mademoiselle Clark.' He bowed
slightly, waiting for her to sit down. 'No doubt you
are surprised to see me here?'

'Yes—I was very surprised to receive your invitation, Monseigneur.' Her voice and her glance were
interrogating, but he was not yet ready to offer her
an explanation of his reason for being there. The wine
was in a cooler by the table; both Jane and her companion watched the waiter uncork it, then pour a little
into Monsieur de Chameral's glass. The tasting of the
wine appeared to be an all-absorbing matter and Jane

was reminded that the French take their wines very seriously indeed.

The first course was served, and it was only when the plates were removed and they were waiting for the second course that Philippe de Chameral spoke, his voice in the main being very quiet, accented, foreign to Jane's ears.

'The children are not happy,' he said, absently tracing the design of the handle of a fork. 'Miss Renshawe is all that I would have considered necessary in a nanny, but the children are obviously adversely affected by the stern measures she sometimes takes with them. For myself, I feel that children require a firm hand....' He allowed his voice to trail away and a frown settled on his dark countenance.

'These two need kindness first, Monseigneur,' Jane said gently. 'I feel you are right when you say that children need a firm hand. They do, for their own good and so that they'll grow up into the kind of people who'll be liked and respected. But this case is a little different, don't you think? Firmness can come later, should come later, when they've had time to forget the tragedy that's affecting them at the present time.' Her companion said nothing, he merely looked at her in a curious kind of way, as if he were learning something of vital importance from her. 'It isn't only their loss—a double one, remember—but the upheaval of coming away from familiar surroundings. The home in which they've been brought up possesses the security of what is familiar. They've been uprooted, brought here to a strange country where everything is totally different, even the climate and, of course, the people. Their guardian is a strange man, their nanny a strange woman. . . .' Jane shook her head, pain darkening her eyes. 'If someone doesn't even give them kindness, Monseigneur, then what have they got left?'

Unknown to herself Jane's eyes were far too bright, her mouth quivering convulsively. 'If you could have found someone younger, perhaps, and with a—softer nature. . . .' Again she trailed off, aware suddenly that she ought not to be speaking in this disparaging way about the children's nanny.

He was thoughtful, absently staring at the vocalist who had appeared and was standing on the dais where the band was playing.

'Have you no idea why I asked you to dine with me, Miss Clark?' he said at last, and Jane glanced up, her eyes questioning. 'I have told Miss Renshawe that she is not suitable.'

'You have?' Jane stared, wondering if he had already found someone else.

And then, with a flash of insight which she realised should have come to her at once, she knew why she was here, dining with the children's uncle, at his invitation.

'Yes, I have. She insists on keeping me to the terms of our contract, which was that there would be a three-month trial. I shall pay her, naturally.' A small pause followed, but Jane did not have long to wait for what she was expecting to hear. 'I am hoping, Miss Clark, that you will consider taking up the post of nanny to Tamsin and Barry.'

She was silent, wishing she were somewhere else, for the dining-table of an hotel did not seem to be the place for making a decision of this kind. Strangely, it had not occurred to her to voice any quick refusal.

She cared about those two children and felt that in some way fate had thrown them together for a purpose. Don did not want her; he had hinted, quite strongly, that he wanted the house and contents sold in order that he could take his share. He wanted a divorce; there was no possibility of reconciliation. So what was there to keep her in England? Again she wished she were somewhere else. She was being rushed into a decision influenced by the desperate plight of the Scott children, but were there any snags? One did not precipitate oneself into a totally new life without at least some prior consideration.

And yet within less than thirty seconds she was hearing herself say,

'I'll accept the post, Monseigneur. When would you like me to start?'

He leant back in his chair, and it was only then, when she heard him draw a long breath, that she fully realised just how anxious he had been.

He looked at her.

'I think it is I who should ask: when can you come, Miss Clark?'

Yes, that was the more sensible way, she had to admit.

'I'd have to go home first,' she began.

'Certainly,' he agreed.

'I suppose....' Jane began to calculate, aware that she was creating a state of urgency that was not necessary, since the children's minds could be put at rest merely by their uncle's being in a position to tell them that Miss Clark was coming soon. 'I should say that a week would be enough. There isn't much to do, not really.'

Philippe de Chameral's glance was swift, and strange.

'A week, mademoiselle? You will surely have to give you employers some notice?'

She coloured, lowering her head quickly. It had entirely slipped her memory that she had led him to believe that she worked for a living.

'Yes—of course. Er—perhaps we had better say a fortnight, I th-think my—employer would be satisfied with one week's notice.'

'I leave it to you, then. The main thing is that it's settled that you take up the post as nanny to my niece and nephew.' He paused a moment, and then, 'You have parents? You might like me to write to them?'

Jane shook her head.

'I have no parents,' she said.

'You're young to have lost your parents. You have brothers and sisters?'

Again she shook her head.

'No, I've no—no relations.' Her eyes smarted suddenly. No relations. . . . Don was already being considered as a nonentity in her life. It was incredible, like something that happens to others but never to oneself.

'I'm sorry,' her companion was saying, but went on to add, his voice cool and clipped and alien-sounding. 'That circumstance does make things easier for you, mademoiselle. You have a home of your own?'

'I share a home.' How easily that had come to her lips!

'I see. Well, it is all settled. You'll receive all expenses, naturally. Perhaps my secretary at the refinery will make a rough assessment and I can advance you some money.'

'There's no need, Monsieur de Chameral,' she said. 'It will do later.' She would have some money from the sale of the furniture, she thought.

'As you wish.' He was beckoning the waiter to fill up their glasses. 'I can now tell the children that you are coming back to them.'

'Have they been very unhappy?' she asked, a tremor in her voice.

'Very. We've had tears every day since you went. I don't believe they would ever have settled if you were unable to come back to them.'

Jane blushed at the compliment but said nothing, and for the remainder of the meal she and her companion talked of inconsequential things, he asking how she liked the hotel, and Jane, encouraged by the slight thawing of his cool detachment, venturing the odd question about his estate, and the refinery.

Jane stood in the middle of the room staring at her husband,

'It's all off, you say? You and Gina have parted, for good?'

Don swallowed, turning from his wife's disbelieving eyes.

'We quarrelled, badly, over something she did——' He broke off, swallowing again. Jane, knowing him so well, saw at once that he was heartbreakingly cut up by the quarrel. 'I don't want to go into it,' he said bitterly. 'It's enough that we've parted, for good.' He came round, to look directly into Jane's bewildered eyes. 'You and I—can we——? I mean, there's no sense in our separating now, is there?'

For a long while she found no answer. Her emotions were distorted, her thoughts shooting off at a tangent as, one moment, her heart rejoiced at the idea of having her husband back and resuming the happy existence she had known before Gina came into Don's life, yet the next moment seeing those two little children, needing her, and already having had the assurance from their guardian that she would be with them soon. She had not told Don of the job in Mauritius yet, and it was natural that he had concluded she was home for good. At last she spoke, but her faltering words gave clear evidence of the turmoil and uncertainty of her mind.

'It—it so happens, Don, that—that I got myself a—a job while I was in Mauritius. I came home only to see you and find out what your plans were for selling up.' She was pale, confused, but never for one moment were those two children out of her mind. In the cold unemotional light of need, theirs was far greater than either her own or that of her husband.

'Got yourself a job?' he frowned. 'But how? Where?'

'As nanny to the children I took over. Monsieur de Chameral offered the job to me and I accepted, feeling I no longer had any ties here.' She desperately wanted her husband, and tears welled up in her eyes because of the turmoil within her. To have a glorious reunion, to hear him say he loved her....

Where were her thoughts taking her? Along a road of dreams which did not exist except in her imagination. For Don did not love her; he still loved Gina, and Jane suddenly knew 'that if the girl were to change her mind and want him back, he would go running to her, forgetting all else in his eagerness and relief.

She looked at him and saw that some of the colour

had drifted from his face. His voice was unsteady when he spoke.

'You mean—you'd go all that way—and leave me?'

Jane shook her head and cried distractedly.

'I don't know, Don—I feel it's my duty—I *know* it's my duty!'

'Your duty?' He seemed amazed. 'Your first duty is to me, surely?'

'To you?' It was Jane's turn to look amazed. Something snapped, impelling her to say,

'Did you think of your duty to me—when you decided to make your life with Gina?'

He turned from her, his shoulders drooping. She waited, vaguely wondering if he would plead with her, as she had pleaded with him, imploring him to give Gina up. He said, over his shoulder,

'I've come back, haven't I? It's what you wanted. You love me, I know it, so you'll give up the idea of this job; it's only logical that you will.'

There was hostile arrogance in his manner, and a confidence that triggered off her anger.

'I'm taking the job,' she told him decisively, and at that he swung around, his eyes glinting.

'You won't! I shan't let you—I can get that Frenchman's address from Nora and write to him——'

'You won't get the address from Nora,' broke in his wife. 'She's thoroughly disgusted with your behaviour and approves of my decision to go to Mauritius and take up this post.'

'You've said things about me—to Nora?'

'It was you who suggested I should confide,' she was quick to remind him.

He nodded sulkily.

'Things were different then. I thought my life was settled.' He sounded dejected now, and hopeless. 'Don't leave me, Jane,' he begged. 'I——' He stopped, choked by emotion. 'I can't be alone, Jane, *I can't live alone*!'

She turned aside, for suddenly she wanted to go to him, to put her arms around him, to comfort him. He had done wrong, had made her unhappy, but she still loved him.

'If it wasn't for the children——,' she began, when Don interrupted her.

'They don't come before me, Jane.'

Silence. What was there to be gained by voicing the angry retort that came to her lips? Yes, he had put Gina before his wife, but he was now bitterly regretting it.

'It isn't only the children,' she said, pale but resolute all at once. 'Although they're the most important, naturally. I made a firm promise to Monsieur de Chameral that I'd return to Mauritius, I can't break that promise, Don.'

'Certainly you can! You've only to write saying you've changed your mind. I'll bet he's half expecting it, anyway!'

'It so happens,' said Jane slowly, 'that I don't want to change my mind. The job's one that appeals to me. It's going to make two children happy, for one thing. For another it's going to take a load off their guardian's mind. And lastly, it gives me an opportunity of saving for my future. The salary's very good indeed.'

Don had been staring through the window, but now he faced her saying curiously,

'How much are you getting?'

'That,' answered Jane tartly, 'is my business.'

'Jane ... you don't need to save for your future. I'm your husband. Let's start again——'

'I can't go back on my word, Don!' She had veered from the path of decisions, for it would be so easy to stay with her husband, and to hope that one day—perhaps quite soon—he would forget Gina altogether and love his wife again. 'You're making it so difficult for me!'

He looked strangely at her.

'Which would you rather do—go away or stay here, with me?'

She closed her eyes tightly, torn apart by duty and desire. He knew she would rather stay, knew she loved him as much now as on the day she married him.

'I m-must go,' she faltered. 'I'd hate myself all my life if I let those little children down.' She thought of Miss Renshawe, and felt that Philippe de Chameral, though loath to do it, would probably retain the woman's services after all. 'I must go!' cried Jane distractedly. 'I *must*!'

'But in your heart you want to stay.'

She nodded, unable to voice a lie.

'Yes,' she whispered, 'I want to stay.' A shuddering sigh that was more like a sob escaped her and the next moment she was in her husband's arms, weeping on his shoulder.

'Jane dear, please stay with me.' So gentle his voice, and persuasive. 'I've made a mistake, but it's all over now. I'll never let you down again—please believe me.' He held her from him, and dried her eyes with his handkerchief. 'You'll stay,' he said, and a smile of confidence hovered on his lips. 'You'll stay because you love me.'

Jane drew away. To both her own surprise and Don's she was shaking her head.

'I must heed my conscience,' she told him quietly. 'I do love you, Don, and want to stay, but I'm not going to. The children's father might be found, and when he is he might just want to have them with him. If that should be the case then I'd be free——' She looked at him through a mist of tears. 'If and when I'm free, Don, I'll come back to you—— No, please don't argue or plead. I've made my decision and it stands.'

'You'll let me write to you, then?' he said, but again Jane shook her head.

'I don't want you to write, Don.'

'Why?' he demanded. 'Why can't I write to you?'

'Because,' answered Jane quietly, 'Monsieur de Chameral doesn't know I'm a married woman.' She went on to explain how she had come to drop her married status, thinking it would be only temporary. 'I can't now say I'm married, can I? Monsieur de Chameral is not the kind of man to overlook deliberate deceit.'

'So if I do write I must put Miss on the envelope, must I?'

She said again that she would prefer him not to write at all.

'I might be away for no more than a few weeks,' she said. 'Please don't write, Don. I'd much rather you didn't.'

He shook his head determinedly.

'I shall write,' he said firmly. 'I must keep in contact with you. However, I'll remember to put Miss on the envelope each time.'

★

The air was filled with the delightful fragrance of frangipani; insects hummed among the flowers, a Mascarene swallow flew about uttering its familiar *sreeleelee*! call before settling on a huge, shady tamarind tree.

Jane was strolling along the path leading to the pool, her swim-suit in her hand, a towel under her arm.

A month had sped by, a month of adjustment both for Jane and her young charges. They were allowed to stay at home for a fortnight after Jane's return to the chateau, after which their guardian arranged for them to start school. Bhoosan took them each morning and brought them back when school was over. This left Jane with a good deal of free time which she spent profitably in exploring her surroundings and in getting to know the whole staff working at the chateau. She also got to know the girl Yvette, but for some reason she could not get along with her. From the first the girl had seemed resentful of Jane's presence; she seemed even more resentful of the children. Jane had once heard her say to Philippe,

'Darling, are you going to keep them permanently?'

'Perhaps, my dear. Depends on whether or not their father wants them—if he is found, that is.'

'I can't say that I want a ready-made family,' Yvette had said candidly. 'Must you have them, Philippe? Surely they have other relations who would be willing to take them. Besides, they'd be happier in their own country.'

'It's my duty to have them, Yvette.'

'Duty?' The girl's voice had sharpened a little. 'I can't see that, Philippe. After all, you're so distantly related that it's scarcely any relationship at all. In fact,

I don't know why you've let them call you uncle.'

'What else would they call me?' he had wanted to know.

'They shouldn't be here at all,' Yvette had said, but Philippe had merely smiled, a circumstance that surprised Jane, who at the time had been sitting on the lawn, while the two sat on the verandah of the drawing-room, both fully aware that she could overhear their conversation. From the first Jane had been surprised by Philippe's attitude towards Yvette, for whereas she would have expected him to be a stern, masterful man when it came to his dealings with the woman whom every one assumed would become his wife, he was in fact, both tolerant and indulgent, which led Jane to believe that he must be very much in love with the girl.

However, they weren't yet engaged, though Yvette acted at times as if they were not merely engaged but married. She would saunter about the house and gardens, giving orders to the servants—this when Philippe was out, working in his office at the refinery. Jane supposed that Yvette was finding little with which to occupy herself—having no need to work— and therefore she spent a good deal of her time at the chateau, often arriving after lunch and remaining until Philippe came home at about five-thirty. She sometimes came to dinner, and Jane would naturally be reminded of those times when she herself had dined in luxury with the owner of the chateau. Since she had become an employee she was not now invited to dine with Philippe, and normally she had her evening meal brought up to her private sitting-room.

Don had written every week and Jane had answered.

She always felt unsettled for a couple of days after the arrival of a letter and began to wish she had been firmer and insisted on withholding her address from him. She upset herself by imagining him arriving home of an evening and having to cook himself a meal, then perhaps clean a room or two and at the week-ends doing his washing and ironing. Repeatedly he said he had made a mistake in falling for Gina, and it was plain by his letters that he was unhappy, and Jane would often find herself praying that Mr Scott would soon be found and that, when he was, he would want his children living with him. Jane would then be free to return to Don, to begin again as he wanted her to. Perhaps they'd start a family, which had been Jane's desire for the past year. It was Don who kept on saying,

'Let's have some more time to ourselves, love. There'll be a lot of our lives taken up with rearing a family. I want you to myself for at least another couple of years.'

The last letter from Don had ended with,

'I miss you, Jane—and I know now that it's you I love, that there never has been anyone else. You were right, darling, when you said it was infatuation I felt for Gina. Come back to me soon, I'm so terribly lonely without you.'

Jane had shed tears when she read the letter and had been depressed for the whole day, desperately wishing that the children's father would be found quickly. Yet immediately on this desire came the question of how Barry and Tamsin would react to yet another upheaval in their lives. They had become settled, contented, happy, having regained that sense of security which is of such vital importance in any child's life. They had already made a few friends among the Indo-Mauritians, the Creoles and others who attended the school.

Having reached the swimming-pool, Jane went into one of the changing rooms to undress; she emerged five minutes later to find that her employer was in the pool.

She stood for a few seconds before turning back to the changing room. Her employer called and she swung around, absurdly self-conscious because she was so scantily clad.

'Aren't you coming in, mademoiselle?' he asked.

'I ... Well, I thought you might not want me using the pool at the same time as you, Monseigneur.'

'Come on in. It's delightfully invigorating.'

She still hesitated, but he beckoned and she dived in, keeping her distance from him. The water was gloriously cool and as she swam about an unexpected sense of happiness swept over her. There was a certain element of companionship in the very fact of her employer's being in the pool with her. It would seem that, for the moment anyway, he was dropping the air of superiority which he invariably adopted towards her.

They came out together; she watched with a sort of selfconscious interest the changing play of his expression as—for the first time that she had noticed—his steely grey eyes flickered over her slender form, from the slim ankles and shapely legs to her tiny waist and higher, where the delicate curves were seductively outlined against the clinging wetness of her costume.

A strange silence ensued, with a hint of tension in

the air ... and the presence of something else ... as profound as it was nebulous. Jane swallowed convulsively, aware of her fluctuating colour, aware that her pose was one of nervous unease because of his eyes upon her, concentrated now and fixed. Her own eyes went with a sort of shy hesitancy to his muscular body, taking in the deep Arab-brown skin, the hair on his chest, curling and holding water droplets, the powerful shoulders, the narrow waist and thighs. ... He was far too attractively masculine. ... He had everything, looks, physique, charm, and the sort of distinguished self-confidence that comes to a man only with maturity. She turned away, bewildered by her thoughts, angry that the man had aroused her interest in him. She tried to supplant the picture by one of her husband ... and incredible as it seemed, she found it impossible to focus Don's features clearly in her mind.

'I've—I've left my clothes in—in there,' she stammered, at length.

'Aren't you going into the pool again?' he wanted to know.

She shook her head.

'I don't think so, Monseigneur, I've some jobs to do.'

'Jobs?'

'There's some mending for the children.' She smiled ruefully. 'Barry tore his shorts climbing a tree.'

'Buy him some new ones. ...' His voice trailed off and, turning her head to follow the direction of his gaze, Jane encountered the hostile stare of Yvette as she strolled towards the pool. She was dressed in a sun-dress of expensive, embroidered linen, with diamonds sparkling on her wrist and fingers. Her dark hair was long and faintly waved, a silken cloak for her bare, sun-tanned shoulders. Tall and assured, she was the picture of elegance and good taste, and Jane felt inadequate all at once, inferior.

'Well, I didn't expect to find you at home, Philippe. Aren't you going to the refinery today?' She ignored Jane completely, even turning her back on her as she spoke to Philippe. Jane, colouring under the deliberate snub, departed silently, seeking the haven offered by the changing-hut.

Yvette came to her later, when Philippe had gone to his study.

'Do you often use the pool at the same time as Monsieur de Chameral?' The dark eyes swung insolently from Jane's face to her feet and back again.

'No, that was the first time.' At the stiff politeness in her voice the other girl's eyes glinted and her mouth went tight.

'I should have thought, Miss Clark, that you would have realised that a servant is not normally allowed to use the swimming-pool at all, much less should she take the liberty of using it at the same time as her employer.'

'Monsieur de Chameral invited me to use it.' Jane's voice was still stiffly polite, but she was marvelling at her control, for the girl's whole attitude was unnecessarily arrogant and aggressive.

'I expect he could not do otherwise, when you were there, undressed and ready to go in.' Yvette paused, but Jane decided that silence would serve her best and after a moment the girl went on, 'When I'm mistress here there'll have to be a change, Miss Clark. I'm warning you in advance that I shall demand total respect from you, and if I don't get it then you'll be replaced.'

This naturally brought a wave of colour to Jane's cheeks—angry colour, and it was only the thought of the children that prevented her from giving the girl a piece of her mind. All she said was.

'We shall leave it until you *are* the mistress here, Miss Sutcliffe.'

The girl strode away, leaving Jane standing on the patio where she had been busy with secateurs, cutting away dead twigs and leaves from a bougainvillaea vine.

CHAPTER FOUR

THE sky was deep purple, and spangled by stars; the talcum-soft beach was deserted except for a couple in the distance, strolling along arm in arm, their heads close together. Jane stopped and found a seat on a small boulder, savouring the deep intensity of the tropical silence. She wondered what the island had been like before Domingo Ferandez landed on it only four hundred and fifty years ago. It must have been a veritable paradise, since it was little less than that now. The Dutch had come next, introducing the sugar cane, which now provided ninety per cent of the island's income. Mauritius was not called 'the sugar pearl of the Indian Ocean' for nothing, Jane had soon learned. Her employer was in sugar in a big way, but there were many others like him, some French, others English.

Another presence close by disturbed the soporific tranquillity of Jane's mind and she turned her head. She sat very still, glad of the deep shadows cast by the lovely bending casuarina trees along the shore. Philippe and Yvette.... The girl was staying at the chateau for a fortnight, her parents having gone to the Seychelles for a holiday. There seemed to be no reason why Yvette could not have stayed in her own home, since her father employed several Creole servants. But she had suggested she come to the chateau and Philippe had raised no objection.

Yvette's attitude towards Jane became more rudely

arrogant and supercilious than ever, and Jane became
fully resigned to leaving Philippe's employ once he and
Yvette were married. Jane only hoped that the
children's father would turn up in time, because if
he didn't she would once again find herself in the position of having to make a choice—to stay or to leave.
She felt at times that she could never stay, not with
Yvette as her employer's wife, but on the other hand
she could not even visualise leaving the children. Yvette
disliked them, though she was exceedingly careful not
to let Philippe know. However, Jane felt instinctively
that very little escaped him, and that he was well aware
that Yvette had no time for Barry and Tamsin. She
had said she did not want a ready-made family, but
that was as far as she had gone where Philippe was
concerned. By some clever and subtle method she
seemed always to cover up her impatience with the
children, but Jane, watching her whenever she was
alone with them, had seen just how short she could be,
or how easily she could pretend not to hear when one
or other of them spoke to her. The outcome of this
was, quite naturally, that the children grew to dislike
her, and they often said to Jane,

'We don't want Miss Sutcliffe here. It's nicer when
she goes home.'

Jane had allowed these comments to pass, feeling
it was better not to let the children think that Yvette
had any important place at the chateau. Soon enough
to disillusion them, if they had to be disillusioned. For
the present they were happy, and settled, having regained that feeling of security that children need, and
which is second only to love.

'Philippe....' The voice was a silky purr, as seductive as a breeze caressing a virgin shore.

'Yes, dear?'

'It's two years now since Edwin died. Don't you think it's enough time?'

A silence followed, with Jane fervently wishing she could move away without being seen. She was in a quandary, aware that the couple had stopped not far from where she sat. Should she get up and go at once—or should she remain here, in the shadows, until they moved on again? She felt she should move, but felt embarrassed because she would have to speak to them, and perhaps have to explain how she came to be here. She had wanted to be alone, to savour the magic and the mystery of the night, to stroll beneath the canopy of stars and stand now and then, to look up and see how many constellations she could identify.

'Perhaps it is enough time.' The voice of her employer drifted to Jane over the crystal clear air, and at his next words her eyes widened to their full extent. 'I made the promise, so I must marry you, mustn't I?'

What did it mean? Was Yvette a widow, having been married to this Edwin, who had died two years ago? But no, Yvette couldn't be a widow, because she had the same surname as her parents. Besides, Meri would have surely mentioned it when she was talking about Yvette, and her probable marriage to Philippe. This promise ...?

'You don't love me.' Complaint in Yvette's voice, but it was still a silken purr for all that.

'I guess people in our position can get along very

well without love.' The deep, masculine voice was a quiet drawl now, and unfathomable. 'When would you like to be married?'

'The children, Philippe? You won't expect me to have them in our home, once we are married?'

'I'm afraid,' he said, still in that strange, unfathomable tone of voice, 'that they are here for good.'

'For good! But their father—he must be somewhere! I thought the British police were searching for him?'

A strange silence ensued before Philippe said,

'He is dead, Yvette, and so you see I am responsible for the children until they're grown up.'

'Dead?' Yvette's tone had changed dramatically, the one word being almost spat out. 'Dead—how do you know?'

'I have been informed. . . .' Jane heard no more, because the couple were walking on and she suspected that it was Yvette who had begun to stride away and that Philippe was following in her wake.

Dead. . . . So the children had no one of their own. . . . A frown creased Jane's forehead, her employer's last words repeating themselves in her brain. 'I have been informed. . . .'

How had he been informed? And why had he not mentioned it to her? Another thought quite naturally came to her: She had hoped soon to be free to return to her husband, had optimistically hoped that Mr Scott would be found and that he would want his children. But now. . . . What exactly was her position here? If Philippe and Yvette married in the near future—and it seemed likely, unless of course Yvette refused to have the children—then she, Jane, would have that choice to make. She would have to leave, she decided. And the thought brought an instant smile to her lips. She could return to her husband. But swift as an arrow shot from a bow the idea was erased as her tender gentle heart went out to Barry and Tamsin. She could not leave them to the mercy of Yvette, who would most likely find another nanny ... one rather like Miss Renshawe.

Jane rose at last, her spirits as low as they possibly could be. Life was all wrong suddenly, with many difficulties and complications. She had felt so at peace when, such a short time ago, she had come out here, and now her mind was in turmoil and she could not even think clearly, either about the present or the future. She supposed it was not at all sensible to put the children first; she had her own life to live and she was married. Her desire was to be with her husband, whom she loved.... Jane's thoughts trailed and her heart felt that the weight which had dropped upon it would never lift again. It was no use telling herself that life would ever be the same as it was before. Don did not love her and that was that. Yes, she wanted to be with him, but would she ever be happy, knowing that if Gina had not thrown him over then she, his wife, would never have got him back? There would have been a divorce and he would have married the woman he loved.

A shuddering sigh escaped her as she walked along the deserted beach. She felt lost and lonely, and she was floundering in a whirlpool of uncertainty. She began thinking again of Philippe's words about a promise. He had obviously made a promise to marry Yvette, and yet they were not engaged. How strange it all was!

Well, decided Jane at last as she entered the grounds of the chateau, it was none of her business and she was gaining nothing by trying to solve what, to her appeared to be a mystery.

Nevertheless, she would not have been human if her curiosity had not led her eventually to put a tentative question to Meri. She and the girl were in the garden, Meri holding a basket in one hand and a pair of scissors in the other. She was cutting flowers for the house. Her ready smile was encouraging and after chatting to her for a few minutes about unimportant things Jane said, hoping she sounded casual,

'Did Miss Sutcliffe have a brother? I heard her mention someone called Edwin, who had died two years ago.'

Meri was snipping a rose; she placed it in the basket before answering Jane's question, and even when she did speak there was a noticeable hesitation which made Jane regret having let her curiosity get the better of her.

'He was her fiancé,' said Meri. 'He died in an accident—as the result of it, that is.' She paused a moment. 'No one ever speaks about it——'

'I'm sorry,' broke in Jane quickly. 'I didn't know there'd been an accident.'

Again there was silence and then Meri seemed to feel she ought to enlighten Jane.

'The only reason we don't speak about it is because Monseigneur overheard some of us discussing it and he became very angry, saying that servants ought not to gossip about their employers. He was right, of course.'

'Yes, he was.'

'But I will tell you, because I know you won't repeat
it. Mr Edwin was Monseigneur's best friend. He once
saved Monseigneur's life—he got cramp while swimming and would have drowned. Monseigneur naturally
felt he owed him a lot and when Mr Edwin was dying
in hospital he begged Monseigneur to take care of
Miss Sutcliffe.' Meri paused again, and mechanically
cut another flower. Jane waited, her attention diverted
fleetingly by a parakeet which flew past her and settled
in the tallest branches of a 'marmalade box' tree where
it sat preening its gleaming, emerald green feathers.
'Mr Edwin was madly in love with Miss Sutcliffe....'
Again a pause, as if Meri were carefully choosing her
words. 'I don't know if Miss Sutcliffe was as madly
in love with him.' She twisted round to face Jane as
she added, her forehead creased in a frown, 'She always
seemed to like Monseigneur—and—and I felt she was
wishing she were engaged to him instead. But at that
time he didn't even notice her very much at all. Mr
Edwin was in a sort of frantic state at the end—the
day before he died, and he begged Monseigneur to
marry Miss Sutcliffe. You see, I think he knew all the
time that she liked his friend better.... It was all very
sad. Monseigneur made the promise, because he
wanted his friend to be happy in his last few hours on
earth.' Meri leant forward and snipped off a yellow
hibiscus flower, which she held in her hand, twisting
the stem between her fingers. 'The doctor, who is
also a great friend of Monseigneur, said that Mr Edwin would die in agony of mind if he wasn't given the
promise.'

Jane's glance moved presently from the girl's pained
countenance to the basket of flowers she held over

her arm. But Jane's eyes were unseeing of the beaut
there; all she did see was the picture created in he
mind by what she had just been told.

'How very sad it was,' she murmured at last.

'Miss Sutcliffe has got over it, though. I think sh
is very happy now that she is liked by Monseigneur.'

'You once said that it was *thought* that Monseigneu
and Miss Sutcliffe would marry. You weren't absolutel
sure.'

Meri shook her head.

'No, because we sometimes wonder if Monseigneu
would like to break the promise. You see, he neve
bothered with a woman before; we all thought he wa
a confirmed bachelor.'

'Perhaps he was, but I feel sure he will keep th
promise he made to his dying friend.'

'I believe you are right, Miss Clark, and they wil
marry one day, perhaps quite soon.'

Jane just had to say,

'Miss Sutcliffe seems to have difficulty in gettin
used to the children.'

'Yes, I have noticed and I am troubled sometime
because she doesn't seem to like them. She has neve
been used to children, you see——' Meri shrugge
expressively, and bent to cut another rose. 'Miss Sut
cliffe will probably soon get to like them,' she ended
but in a tone that was not at all convincing.

Later in the day Philippe sent for Jane to ask he
about the children. He did this about once a week
he asked her if she was happy at the same time, and i
there was anything that she wanted, or that did no
suit her. Meri had already told Jane of his concern fo

the welfare of those in his employ, and although his manner with Jane was cool and detached, there was no doubt in her mind that he really cared about her contentment and happiness regarding her job.

After he had asked a few questions and been given the answers he said, his whole attention appearing to be on the pen he was holding and at which he was staring intently,

'The children's father ... he is dead.' Philippe's voice seemed different in some subtle, indefinable way. Nerves tingled along Jane's spine; she asked herself why he was not looking at her as he spoke such vitally important words. She repeated softly,

'Dead, Monseigneur?'

He nodded his head.

'I'm afraid so.'

'You—er—must have heard from the English police?' She thought of Nora, who had said in her letter received only last week,

'No sign of Mr Scott, but we did think it would be difficult to locate him if he was abroad. However, no news is good news, so we might have a surprise one day and find that he has been found.'

'Yes, I have.' Philippe still stared at the pen he held.

'So this means that you'll have them permanently?'

'Of course. I can't let them go now. They're settled and happy and although I'd have let them go to their father—if he had wanted them, that is—I shan't let them go anywhere now.' There was a little more expression in his voice—a certain forcefulness, in fact, almost as if he were determined that Jane should keep in mind the fact that they were to reside permanently at the Chateau de Chameral. She thought: he's making sure that I fully understand that I'm to stay here indefinitely.

But what of her promise to Don? She had said she would return as soon as she could, giving him to understand that she definitely would return one day ... when the children's father was found.

'It's very sad that Barry and Tamsin should be orphaned at their age.' No comment from her employer and she added, looking curiously at him, 'How did Mr Scott meet his death?'

'I have no idea.' The voice was sharp now and clearly repressive. Jane realised that he was not intending to answer any more questions.

For the next few minutes he talked about other things, but it was plain that his thoughts were a long way off and it was a relief to Jane when at last he said,

'There doesn't seem to be anything else, so you may go.'

In the corridor she met Yvette and the girl barred her way as she would have walked past her.

'You've been with Monsieur de Chameral for some time. What were you talking about?'

Jane stared, unable to believe her ears.

'That's a strange question to ask, Miss Sutcliffe,' she returned coolly.

Yvette coloured but set her mouth, at the same time allowing her eyes to flick over Jane with an arrogant expression.

'Is there any reason why you shouldn't tell me what you were talking about, Miss Clark?' Her manner was suggestive of patronage, as if she were reminding Jane of her inferior position in the household. Jane paused, determinedly suppressing the anger that was rising as a result of this girl's attitude towards her. She had no desire to give Yvette an excuse for running to Philippe with tales to carry. She said at last, in a quiet voice untinged with any hint of hostility,

'None at all, Miss Sutcliffe. We talked about the children. Monsieur de Chameral often sends for me and asks about them.'

'His concern's a matter of amazement to me.' The girl spoke reflectively, as if she were more absorbed in thought than in what she was saying. 'You must know that they aren't in any way related.'

'I believe they are related, though distantly——'

'There is no blood tie at all!' Almost vicious the tone suddenly and once again Yvette appeared to be speaking her thoughts aloud. 'Did he tell you that their father is dead?' The clear pale brow creased in a frown and the beautiful lips were marred by compression.

'Yes,' replied Jane, 'he did tell me.'

'It means that the children are to stay here indefinitely?'

'I was given to understand that, Miss Sutcliffe.' Watching her intently as she spoke, Jane noticed the swift contraction of a muscle in her throat, as if she were affected by some emotion that caused her pain.

'You——?' Yvette's eyes were narrowed as she looked at her. 'Surely you were not expecting to remain here indefinitely?'

'I was to stay until the children's father turned up—if he turned up.'

'And now?'

'I don't know,' Jane thought of Don, and of her

promise to return to him when she was free. Would she ever be free now? she wondered. Perhaps not until the children were grown up and no longer needed her care. The future was nebulous all at once, and only the present seemed to be of any importance.

Jane's thoughts switched to her conversation with Meri, when the Creole girl had hinted that Philippe would like to break the promise he had made to his dying friend, the friend to whom he owed his life. Yet if this were so, why had he allowed Yvette to come for a fortnight? Surely, if he did not want to marry her, he would rather not have her around the house, especially as there was not the least necessity for her to be here, with her own home so close. There was also the question of the girl's dislike for the children; Jane had already decided that Philippe knew that Yvette disliked them, so the case against his having the girl here was even stronger.

It didn't make sense, thought Jane, feeling that if only she could find one small clue the whole mystery would be solved.

Yvette was walking away; Jane watched her for a long moment before turning away herself. Yes, if only one clue could be grasped then everything would fit nicely into place ... including the reason for Philippe's assertion that the children's father was dead. ...

Jane frowned at this thought, because of course the man might be dead. On the other hand, she could not believe that he was.

Jane had intended, when Bhoosan returned, to ask him to take her into Port Louis, as she had some shopping to do for the children. Philippe had said she could have the car whenever he did not want it himself, but Yvette had had it several times since she came to the chateau and Jane would never have ventured the request that she should accompany her, even though she knew that on at least one of those occasions the girl was going into the capital, and on another into Curepipe, where the facilities for shopping were equally as good as in Port Louis. However, when she asked the chauffeur if he would take her to town Jane received the information that he was taking her employer, so she naturally abandoned the idea there and then.

She was in the garden, in a sun outfit of brief shorts and a daring triangle of the same material which covered her just enough for decency. A honey-golden tan already acquired added infinitely to her beauty, and her silky dark hair had been slightly bleached above her forehead, giving the impression of burnished gold threads running through it. She lay on a garden lounger, totally relaxed despite the letter she had just received from her husband, whose complaints of being all alone were strangely far less troublesome to her than before, perhaps because of their repetition.

She had an unopened book on the grass by her side; it was far more pleasant merely to gaze around, slowly, and be able to appreciate the incredible beauty that was everywhere—the scented flowers and bushes, the tall graceful trees, the crystal spray of the fountain, the giant waterlilies, the glowing sky of sapphire blue. She could see the clear sparkling waters of the lagoon, light green in the sunlight. She was very fortunate, she mused, being here, in this luxurious tropical setting. Fate was strange....

Her mind was on her employer all at once; she was

becoming vitally aware of his attractions, and there were times when she found it almost impossible to take her eyes off him. She thought of the time they had swum together, and only a couple of days ago he had reminded her that the pool was for her enjoyment if she wanted to use it. Yvette used it mid-morning and sometimes in the afternoon. She had been in with Philippe, too, on a couple of occasions; Jane had watched them from her bedroom window. Something had stirred within her and she knew that she had felt a tinge of envy of the girl who was so friendly with the noble owner of the lovely chateau.

A movement made her turn her head; she coloured delectably as her employer's dark eyes swept over her scantily-clad figure, their expression inscrutable. It seemed an eternity before he spoke.

'Bhoosan tells me you want to go into town.'

'I did—but you want the car, so——'

'There is ample room for two of us,' he interrupted quietly. He glanced at his watch, then at her state of undress again. 'I can give you about ten minutes, no longer.'

'Thank you—thank you very much, Monseigneur.'

She rose even as he walked away, wondering where Yvette was and if she would have liked to be taken into town with Philippe. Probably not, since if she had she would have spoken to him about it and he would not then have invited Jane to go with him.

She was ready and actually waiting when he came from the verandah in front of his study and walked briskly to the car, arrogance and self-assurance in every step he took. Jane actually experienced a little throb of excitement as, reaching the car, he handed her in, while Bhoosan held open the door at the other side. He was too often in her thoughts, Jane chided herself as he got in and sat down beside her. His image was fleeting, mostly, but persistent for all that, and it came at odd times, as when she was taking a meal with the children, or on her own, pressing or mending their clothes. The image sometimes came when she was writing to Don, intruding into her vision and blotting out that of her husband.

'You are very quiet, Miss Clark.' Her employer's soft voice broke into Jane's reflections and she turned involuntarily, without thinking, and her hair swung right into his face.

'Oh, I'm sorry. . . .' She moved to one side. He merely smiled faintly and she was encouraged to say, 'I was thinking, Monseigneur.'

'Serious thoughts, by the expression in your eyes,' he said.

'Not very serious.' She wondered what he would think were he to know just what her thoughts had been. She looked at his profile, marvelling at the sheer perfection of his features. He disturbed her, in some unfathomable way, and she looked through the window, determined to concentrate on something else. The road they were travelling was through fields of sugar cane, with palms and casuarinas bordering the roadside. Flowers were everywhere—morning glory bushes edging gardens, the lovely African tulip trees with their brilliant crimson blooms, the showy hibiscus in both gold and red.

Philippe spoke again, breaking a long silence, to ask

what it was that she needed, as she had merely told him, the day before, that the children required some new clothes.

'I ask merely to make sure you have enough money,' he added in that attractive, finely-modulated voice. 'You can always open an account in my name, if ever you happen to be short of money when shopping in town.'

She said nothing, sure that she would never do anything like that. But his trust brought warmth to her body, a happy light to her eyes. At first she had considered him stiff, unfeeling, a man whose bachelor existence seemed to have a flavour of selfishness about it; she considered him to be rather too self-sufficient, too smugly secure in his established way of life. She had felt sure he lacked understanding, that he considered himself way above people like herself, but gradually she had come to regard him in a very different light, accepting his arrogance as an inherent trait, his air of superiority as something most attractive, because again it was a part of him, an important characteristic. His smile was made more attractive by the fact of its being seldom seen.

Philippe was speaking, asking again what she needed. She glanced at him quickly, having quite forgotten to answer his question, lost as she was in her musings.

'Tamsin wants underwear and socks, and a couple of pairs of sandals. Barry needs shorts and one or two more T-shirts. And they both need satchels for school. All the children are required to have them now, it seems. Before, it was only the older ones.'

'That's quite a lot of stuff. I'll give you a cheque which you can cash at the bank.' Withdrawing his cheque-book from his pocket, he proceeded to make out a cheque for her. Jane's eyes widened as they caught the amount.

'I shan't be needing anything like this, Monseigneur,' she protested. 'I think perhaps you'd better take it back....' Her voice trailed to silence as she saw his expression.

'You can give me the change,' he told her abruptly. 'Better to have too much than too little.' He glanced at his wrist-watch and after a moment of indecision added, 'We're early. I think I'll be through with my business by about half-past one. Meet me in the lobby of the Stag Hotel at that time and we'll have lunch there.'

Jane stared at his profile, her feelings very mixed. The thought of taking lunch with him was undeniably pleasant; on the other hand, she was in doubt as to how she would feel. Would she be out of her depth? She had dined with him, though, when she first came to his house. Lunching out could not be any different.

She finished all her shopping in plenty of time, then went straight to the hotel where, finding the powder-room, she spent more time on her appearance than she had done since the break with her husband. After washing her face and hands she sat before a large mirror and applied colour to her cheeks and lips, subtly, with care, as she had been taught once by a demonstrator in the cosmetic department of the big store in the town where she and Don lived. With a little pang she remembered the occasion; it was in the late afternoon of her birthday, and Don was taking her to dine and dance. She allowed herself to be used for the demonstration, having been picked out by the girl who was doing it. She had wanted to look nice for her husband ... for Don....

Such happy days ... and so long ago. One should never go back, she had been told by her aunt. Go forwards to gain; go backwards to lose.

Her aunt swore it was good advice, but at the time it had little or no meaning for the young niece to whom she gave it. Now it did have a meaning. She was beginning to accept that her life with Don could never be the same again, that to go back could very well be to lose, as her aunt had declared.

She put her lip rouge and blusher away in her bag and took out a comb. Her hair gleamed, dark beechnut brown laced with honeycomb gold at the front. She liked it! She felt good, and happy, experiencing a little throb of anticipation as she emerged from the powder-room into the lobby and saw Philippe just coming through the swing doors from outside.

He smiled; her whole world was rosy and she refused to ask herself why, or to analyse her feelings, or to think of anything beyond this interlude, when she was to lunch with such a distinguished person as Philippe de Chameral.

'We're both early.' His voice was suave, his grey eyes unguardedly appreciative as they swept over her, from the shining glory of her hair to her animated face, then to the graceful curve of her neck and shoulders, both honey-tanned and contrasting with the white linen sun-dress she was wearing. His eyes roved her figure, exquisitely proportioned from her tiny waist to her shapely ankles. She coloured in the most attractive way, saw to her surprise a touch of humour come to his eyes, and she felt very young.

She gave him a winning smile, murmured a tremulous, 'Yes, we are,' in response to his remark, and the next moment a Creole waiter appeared and they were conducted to the restaurant, and to a table by the window, in a corner where flowers and palms in pots provided seclusion on two sides.

'This is lovely!' The impulsive exclamation caused the waiter to smile. Jane's expression closed as she looked at her employer. Had she said the wrong thing? Was it naïve of her to express her delight like that?

'It is rather attractive, isn't it?' The reassuring words came from Philippe as he took a chair after having seen her seated by the waiter.

It was easy to see that Philippe was regarded with great esteem by the waiters, two of whom were already hovering, waiting for him and Jane to read the menu. The wine list was brought and Philippe took some time over his choice, handing the list back and speaking in French as he made his choice known.

'You managed to get all you wanted?' he enquired of Jane while they were waiting for the first course.

'Yes, it was one of those days when everything was easy.'

He nodded, his eyes flickering from her hair to her eyes.

'May I say how charming you look, Miss Clark? White suits you, especially with that tan you've acquired. You were rather pale when you first came——' He stopped and a slight frown touched his forehead. 'Had you been ill?'

Jane shook her head.

'Not *ill*—no,' she replied, not realising that she had emphasised the word until her companion said,

'Something else, then? You certainly appeared to have something on your mind, something unpleasant.'

She had not expected him to be so perceptive at that time, since she was merely the woman—a stranger —who had agreed to bring his charges over from England. She was in a quandary as to how to answer him, and in the end decided neither to lie nor to be completely honest.

'There was a troublesome little thing that happened not long before I came here. I—brooded on it and so I expect my appearance was affected.' A lightness entered her tone as she added finally, 'Coming here did me the world of good, Monseigneur; I was grateful for the opportunity of having something else to occupy my mind.'

He said after a pause during which his eyes had never left her face,

'You speak of a *little* thing. I believe that you are not altogether honest about it, Miss Clark.'

She gave a start, taken aback by his assertion and the cool confident way he had made it.

'It—it's a private matter,' she said presently, an appeal in her tone which she hoped he would respect.

'Of course; I understand, but I am interested nevertheless. You say that coming here did you good. I must agree, because you look so well.' A pause ensued and then he said, 'If ever you feel like confiding, Miss Clark, then do not hesitate to come to me.' Faintly he smiled. 'I believe I'm a more sympathetic listener than may appear on the surface.'

She looked at him in surprise. He was more human than ever before. And he was inviting her confidence and she wondered if the letters she received from her husband had aroused his curiosity. He would see at once that they were in a man's hand; he would know that they came often. With a little access of apprehension she wondered if, in his uncannily perceptive way, he had guessed that she was married. But why should he? A boy-friend, perhaps; yes, he might surmise she had a boy-friend, but there was no reason in the world why he should suspect she had a husband.

CHAPTER FIVE

JANE and the children were having afternoon tea in the garden when Barry said, right out of the blue,

'Miss Sutcliffe's nice now. She was in the car with us when we were coming home from school because Bhoosan stopped to give her a lift because she'd been for a walk and it was a long one and she felt tired, so she put her hand up for Bhoosan to stop and he did and Miss Sutcliffe talked to us and smiled and I liked her, but Tamsin wouldn't smile at her and she doesn't think she's nice but I do.' He stopped for breath, spooning up some jelly at the same time. Jane had seen Yvette get out of the car and had surmised she had been walking and that Bhoosan had stopped to give her a lift.

'What did she say to you, Barry?'

'She said we were nice children and asked me if we liked you and I said yes, and she said did we know you before and I said no but we knew Mrs Davis and Mrs Davis looked after us and——'

'You forgot something,' interrupted Tamsin, her mouth full of cake. 'She asked you if Auntie Jane had a gentleman friend in England, don't you remember?'

'Oh, yes. It was before she asked me if we'd known her before, wasn't it?'

'She asked you that . . .?' Jane's brow creased in a frown. Yvette sometimes picked up the letters after the postman had been. One morning she had cast Jane

an odd sort of glance as she handed her one of them.
It was from Don. 'And now you think she's nice?'

'She was smiling all the time, and she said she would
buy us some chocolate tomorrow.'

It was easy to understand the workings of the girl's
mind! She was making herself agreeable to the children
merely to pump them.

'I don't want any chocolate from her!' flashed Tamsin. 'She isn't nice, so there, Barry!'

'She didn't used to be nice, I know.' Barry's voice
had changed and there was a tinge of doubt in it as
he added, 'She was nicer than she was other times,
wasn't she?'

'I didn't want her to be in the car with us.'

Jane said quietly,

'Never mind, Tamsin. Have some more cake.'

'Can I have some more jelly?' Barry was already
reaching out towards the dish.

'Of course——' Jane glanced up and a ready smile
came to her lips. She helped Barry to his jelly while
at the same time listening to the suave, attractive voice
of her employer,

'What a charming, homely little tea-party. May I
join you?'

'Oh, yes, Uncle Philippe!' from Tamsin in a hurry.
'But there isn't much jelly left! Barry's eaten it all!'

'I never! You had more than me at first!'

'I don't think I shall require any jelly.' There happened to be a garden chair close at hand and Philippe
brought it to the table, sitting opposite to Jane. She
coloured a little at his stare, disconcerted by his un-
disguised attention. She recalled the lunch they had
had together three days ago, when his manner had

changed so noticeably towards her. They had eaten
shark steak, grilled golden brown, then garnished with
shallots and mustard and flamed in brandy, this after
a starter of small fish marinaded in lime juice and
sprinkled with herbs and garlic and fried in butter.
They had drunk heady wine, then coffee and cognac.
Philippe had very plainly enjoyed the meal, which
meant of course that he had enjoyed being with her.
An emotion, a yearning stronger than reason, had
enveloped her that same evening when, meeting him
in the hall of the chateau after Yvette had gone to
bed, she had basked in the warmth of his smile and
thrilled absurdly to the perfectly prosaic manner in
which he had bidden her goodnight.

'So you're off to bed, Miss Clark? You've been for
a late stroll, obviously. Goodnight. Sleep well.'

'Goodnight, Monseigneur,' she had returned shyly.
'Er—yes,' she added confusedly, 'I have been for a
late stroll.'

Several times since then she had been confused when
in his presence and, with his keen perception, it was
reasonable to assume that he was aware of this con-
fusion. What did he think of her? she wondered. Was
he amused? Had he come into contact with her kind
before—young ladies who lost their confidence, being
affected by his overpowering influence? His face had
always been a smooth mask, unreadable, yet by some
indefinable instinct she sensed an underlying interest,
sensed that his thoughts were often with her, even
when she was not anywhere near him. It was a strange
sensation and she began to wonder if it were born of
desire ... desire that he should become really interested
in her as a woman.

He was talking to the children and she listened, thinking that it was a shame he had no children of his own. For contrary to her original opinion, she knew he would make a wonderful father—kind and just, a friend and a protector.

'Uncle Philippe, can we have a party?'

'Why? It isn't anyone's birthday.'

'It is! It's Auntie Jane's——'

'Tamsin dear——'

'It is? When?' Philippe's glance went to Jane's flushed face and he seemed amused at her embarrassment.

'I asked her when it was her birthday and she said it was on Saturday and I said how old is she and she said you never ask a lady how old she is. I think she's twenty-one because nearly all ladies are twenty-one—— Well, all the teachers at my school in England were twenty-one, and Mrs Davis said she was twenty-one when I asked her and my friend's mother said she was twenty-one when I asked her. Do you think Auntie Jane is——?'

'Good lord, Miss Clark, do you have to put up with this sort of chatter all the time? Remind me to double your salary!' Philippe was laughing as he spoke and Jane felt her heart jerk at the attractiveness of him. He so seldom smiled, even, and to see him laugh like that....

'Mrs Davis said I chatter, but I like it and I don't know how to stop!'

'He gets on your nerves,' declared his sister disparagingly. 'Mummy used to say he did.'

'It's better to chatter than to sulk—and you're always sulking!'

Rima, one of the housemaids, appeared before any more was said. She was told by Philippe to bring crockery for him and a fresh pot of tea.

'And sandwiches, Monseigneur?' she asked respectfully.

'Perhaps a couple, Rima, but nothing else.' He waited until the girl had turned away before saying to Jane, 'So you've a birthday coming up? We shall certainly have to think of something.'

'It doesn't matter,' she protested, wishing she had thought before mentioning it to the children. Barry had said, only yesterday,

'A little boy at school is seven today and we all sang to him. It's my birthday just after Christmas. When's yours, Auntie Jane?'

And she had replied,

'It happens to be quite soon, Barry—on Saturday, in fact.' It had never for a moment occurred to her that this situation would be the result.

'Certainly it matters.' Philippe looked across at her with the hint of a smile on his handsome face. 'Yes, Barry, I think we must have a party, just a small one for us four.'

'Great! Can we have it on the beach?'

'I don't see why not.'

Rima returned carrying a tray and for a few minutes the four at the table were quiet. As soon as she had gone Philippe astounded Jane by saying that after the 'party' he and she would dine out somewhere. She stared dazedly, unable to believe her ears.

'But, Monseigneur, you c-can't want to take me—— I mean,' she amended hurriedly, 'there's no need——'

'There is every need,' he broke in gently. 'And as

for what you were going to say about my not wanting to take you out—when you know me a little better you will discover that I never do anything unless I want to do it.'

'You're very kind to me, Monseigneur.' There was a slight catch to her voice, because she was rather full up and because she had been resigned to having her birthday pass without anyone even knowing about it. She met his eyes, eyes that were keen and perceptive; he knew that she was glad that her birthday was not to pass unnoticed. A smile fluttered to her lips and he responded, bringing warmth to her heart. He seemed to guess that she was touched, and a little full up, and he eased the moment for her by a request that she should pour his tea for him. She thought fleetingly of Don, and the times he had taken her out on her birthday, but no real emotion stirred her at the memories.

The tea poured, she put down the pot and picked up the sandwiches. He took one from the plate and put it on the one in front of him. The children were chattering, excited about the party. Barry wanted to know if he could go to the shops to look for a present, but Tamsin said she was going to pick Auntie Jane a bunch of flowers from the garden.

'I haven't any money to buy a present,' Barry said, looking at his uncle. 'Will you please give me some——?'

'Barry!' exclaimed Jane, horrified. 'You do *not* ask for money!'

But to her surprise Philippe only laughed good-humouredly and promised that Barry should have some money and that Bhoosan would take him to the shops.

Jane, hot with embarrassment at the idea of her

employer giving Barry money for a present for her, would have protested, but at that moment Yvette came up, looking cool and lovely in a crisp leaf-green dress of linen, cut low to reveal shapely shoulders and to show off to advantage the beautiful diamond and sapphire necklace she was wearing.

'Philippe! I've been looking for you everywhere! I never expected you to be here, having tea with the children and their—nanny!' No mistaking the intonation when the last word was spoken, or the malevolent expression in the eyes that met Jane's in a prolonged and narrowed stare.

'A pleasant change,' returned Philippe imperturbably as he rose with the intention of giving Yvette his chair. She flung a hand arrogantly and said she was going for a walk.

'I shall see you later, then.' Philippe glanced over her svelte figure with eyes that could only be described as indifferent. 'Dinner will be a little late this evening, as I've some work to do. I shall be in my study until about nine o'clock.'

Yvette frowned heavily. She was angry and some of the colour had left her face, giving it a look of transparency that was far from attractive.

'What time's dinner to be, then?'

'Around half-past nine, or even ten o'clock.'

Yvette's glance went from Philippe to Jane and back again, an ugly line curving her mouth. It was plain that she blamed Jane for the lateness of dinner, since if Philippe were not taking tea with her and the children he would be in his study doing the work which he was intending to do later. Before she had time to speak Barry was saying.

'We're having a tea-party on Saturday! It's Auntie Jane's birthday!'

'A party?' echoed Yvette, her frown deepening.

'Just for us four! It's going to be on the beach!'

'A party for four?' The arched brows lifted fractionally, 'How very exciting.' The sarcasm was of course lost on the children and Barry was soon asking Yvette if she would like to come to the party.

'Then it'll make five!' he added.

'Miss Sutcliffe will have gone to her own home by then, Barry.' Philippe was still standing by his chair, one strong brown hand resting on the back of it. 'She is leaving us on Friday.'

'I could stay till Saturday evening.' Smooth the tone, and faintly challenging.

'Certainly, if you would like to come to the party, Yvette,' was Philippe's gracious rejoinder.

'I'll think about it,' she told him shortly, and a moment later she was gone.

Meri and Rima prepared the party, bringing out a low table and chairs, while Barry and Tamsin helped by carrying cutlery and plates and cups and saucers.

For Jane it was something entirely new and she was happy for the children, but she had to agree with what Meri had said earlier about its not being a real party since there were not enough people. However, the presence of their uncle was a real treat for the children and the absence of other children seemed to trouble them not at all. Barry had been out with Bhoosan, who took him to several shops before Barry managed to get what he wanted. Bhoosan told Jane afterwards that he had never met a child so particular in his choice. He wanted a 'pretty bottle with ribbon tied round it' and he went from one shop to another until he found one. Jane thanked the chauffeur for his patience. He had four children of his own, with the result that he had infinite understanding of their wishes and ideas.

The table certainly looked attractive, with dainty sandwiches, pastries, jellies and a trifle topped by lashings of fresh cream and nuts.

For Jane Philippe's attitude was a revelation. He was a different person altogether from the reserved, aristocratic Frenchman who at first had been almost frighteningly superior. Today he was very human ... and very attractive. But there was something else as well—an attitude of intimacy about him that disturbed her, affecting her senses, sharpening her awareness of him as a man.

Yvette had decided not to come and for that Jane was inexpressibly thankful; the whole thing would have been spoilt for her had the other girl been present.

When the party was over Philippe asked if everyone had enjoyed it. The children declared it to be 'lovely!' and to Jane's surprise they both remembered to thank their uncle for giving it. She herself thanked him, and then they both laughed, aware that a great pretence had been going on.

Later he said,

'We shall have a proper party one day soon, a dinner-party, with perhaps a dozen or so guests.'

She blinked at him.

'You mean—that I shall be there?'

He nodded his head.

'You haven't met anyone, Jane, and it's time you did.'

Jane.... Her heartbeats quickened. Did he *like* her? She thought of Yvette and the promise he had made regarding her; she thought too of Meri's doubts about his wanting to keep that promise.

Yvette was not the girl for him. She was cold and distant, and she did not like children. Philippe ought to be a father; it would be a shame if he never had children of his own. But suddenly Jane was very sure that if he was married to Yvette and he wanted children, then his will would override hers; she would have his children whether she liked it or not.

Night was falling when they left the chateau for the St Geran Hotel in the luxurious car with Philippe at the wheel. Jane was very lovely and feminine in an Edwardian-style evening gown of the delightful and subtle colour of mulled wine. Over it she wore a velvet cape with a large hood draping her shoulders and falling down the back. Her hair gleamed, newly washed and set, and in it she wore a slide with tiny diamonds, a gift from her aunt on her nineteenth birthday.

Philippe was immaculate as usual, attired this evening in a white linen suit which he wore with an air of casual informality. It had a soft, almost draped line but was very masculine for all that. He was every inch a gentleman, thought Jane casting him a sideways glance, a distinguished, noble Frenchman whom she was thrilled to have as her escort. Yet it was natural that her thoughts should stray to her husband, and that she should wonder if he were remembering what day it was, and how she was spending the evening.

Would he be recalling those other evenings that had been so happy? A tiny sigh escaped her and Philippe said quietly,

'What was that for, Jane? Are you not happy?'

'Oh, yes, indeed I am! It was nothing——'

'One does not sigh for nothing,' he broke in gently. 'One usually sighs when memories intrude.'

His perception again! The man was almost omniscient! Jane could find nothing to say to that and for a short time there was silence in the car. And then he spoke again, this time to mention that there was to be dancing at the hotel tonight.

She caught her breath. To dance with him! The idea of having him hold her in his arms.... She felt she was being awakened to a new and exciting life; she was forced to admit that with every meeting with Philippe de Chameral she fell more and more under the spell of his magnetism. Where would it all end? She had made a promise to her husband to return at the earliest possible time, but more and more it was becoming doubtful if she would ever live with him again. Even if she were to leave here she felt she would want to make an entirely new life for herself.

The moon was a great argent sphere by the time they reached the hotel; it was too early to dine and after parking the car Philippe suggested a stroll in the lovely grounds. He took her arm when they reached the beach, and they walked in companionable silence for some time before Jane said, pointing out across the lagoon to the lights on the horizon,

'Doesn't that ship look tempting?'

'Tempting?'

'I'd love to travel on a ship—a really big one.'

'You have never been on a big liner?'

'Never. We didn't have the money for that kind of travel. I surmise that the ship is cruising.'

'It could be on a world cruise.'

'Have you ever been on a world cruise?' They were treading the talcum-soft sand, but now and then Jane put her foot on a piece of coral washed ashore from the reef.

'No, I've never had the time. There's a great deal of work attached to an estate like mine.'

'You enjoy your work, though?'

'Every minute; it's rewarding.' His hand was still on her arm; she was profoundly conscious of it, and of the fact that their bodies touched now and then as they walked along. She glanced skywards, marvelling as always at the splendour of the heavens in this part of the world. A million stars in a sky of deep purple, with clouds like lace or cobweb silk, scarcely real. The moon creating light on the shore and mysterious shadows in the casuarina trees fringing it; the drowsy lagoon, breathing gently against the shore, the distant splash of the sea tumbling over the reef. The romantic lights of the ship on the dark line of the horizon.... It was all too achingly wonderful, a dream from which never to awaken. She was intoxicated, her senses swimming, her mood suddenly reckless. There was no past in her life and no future. This night was eternity and heaven seemed only a breath away.

She had to speak, to break a silence that was becoming unbearable, and her voice was husky because she had to try to hide her feelings.

'It's a most beautiful island, Monseigneur. It's just perfect in every way.'

He turned, and looked down into her face.

'God made Mauritius first,' he quoted, 'and then heaven, heaven being copied from Mauritius.'

'What a beautiful thing to say!'

'Mark Twain said it originally.'

'He visited the island, then?'

'At the end of the century.' He turned without speaking and they began to retrace their steps, going leisurely towards the lights of the hotel. Philippe had taken his hand from her arm, but it came back swiftly as she stood on a rather large piece of coral and twisted on her ankle. It gave her no pain, merely jerking her sideways, against him.

His other arm seemed to come out so naturally that she was in his embrace before she knew it, her soft young body pressed close against his. Neither of them moved; a tremor passed through Jane and her face lifted to his. This was no gentle stirring of a desire, but a wild uncontrolled yearning for physical pleasure and fulfilment, a primitive instinct awakening her from the dream in which her sex life had been suspended since the break with her husband. She knew her nerves were unstrung, that this flame of longing had been ignited only because of the circumstances in which she was in. But she was powerless to regain her sanity ... she had no desire to regain it, for this mad throbbing of her heart was ecstasy exquisitely painful, this craving to be taken and mastered and brought to willing surrender, an emotion beyond rational thought or visions of the consequences.

It was inevitable that he would kiss her; she had tempted with her eyes, her rosy lips seductively parted, her quickened breathing. A great quiver of delight rippled through her whole body as his lips met hers, gentle at first, but as he began to realise she was in a yielding mood his ardour flared and she was swept along on a tide of passion she had never known before. He drew away, his eyes dark in the moonlight.

'Kiss me, Jane!' The imperative command was instantly obeyed and within seconds she was swept once again into the vortex of his passion. It was a revelation to Jane who had thought him cold and unemotional. But he was a man, with all the savage instincts of a passionate nature; she could imagine the untamed mastery he would adopt in his lovemaking, the fire, the violence of his emotions, the savage intensity of his final conquest.

She was afraid suddenly, and tried to draw away, but it proved to be a feeble, fruitless effort because her will failed under the dangerous fascination of his presence.

'Jane ... you're beautiful ... and tempting!' His voice was low, throaty, vibrant with desire unspent.

'Monseigneur, please. ...' Another attempt, as feeble as the last. There was too much to be enjoyed, in this setting of moonlight and starlight, of palms swaying on a white sandy shore caressed by the crystal waters of the lagoon, of intoxicating perfumes invading the soft balmy air.

'Please ... what?' Was there a hint of humour in the voice, a voice that had lost much of its passion? The pause following his words was tense, for Jane felt she had been taken to the very portal of heaven, only to have the door slammed in her face. 'Do you want to remain out here for a while?' he queried at length, when she did not speak.

He seemed cold all at once; Jane felt repulsed, staggered by the swift, dramatic change that had come over him, for he was now in full control of his emotions and the scene of a moment ago might never have occurred. His manner was a knife-thrust in her heart. She managed to speak, but merely to utter a stumbling negative.

'N-no....'

'Then let us go and eat.' He was suave and dignified, politely gracious, but that was all. They walked in silence; Jane wanted to say something, to bring his mind back to what had just gone, but no suitable words came to her lips.

They entered the restaurant and instantly a waiter was there, to conduct them to a table where they had a good view of the instrumentalists who were to play for the dancers. For Jane the evening had fallen flat. Her one nagging emotion was what he must be thinking of her—to reciprocate so easily, practically to offer herself to him, for that was what it must have seemed like. Embarrassment, regret, self-shame ... all these combined to engulf her in a web of sheer misery and she would have given anything to run away, far, far away from this idyllic island ... and find the comfort that she knew her husband was willing to give her. He *wanted* her. Here, she was wanted only by the children, and by her employer only because she looked after them so well.

'You are very quiet, Jane.' His voice drifted into her musings a few minutes after they had sat down. The waiter had taken her cloak, and she looked exquisite in the Edwardian dress, sitting upright in her chair, regal, like a queen, the centre of everyone's interest.

Yes, she would not have been all woman had she been unaware of the looks of admiration cast her way, mainly by the men. The women looked at Philippe who, unlike Jane, seemed totally oblivious of any interest in himself. The women's glances did inevitably move to his companion, envious glances but not malicious, as Yvette's invariably were.

'I—I was interested in—in—everything.' Tears were close and a painful lump had settled in her throat. Her eyes, large and wistful and faintly accusing, looked into his, seeing an enigmatic, unchanging expression which only served to increase her regret for what had happened. He was hating the fact of his own weakness—perhaps he was putting the entire blame on her. She *was* to blame, she supposed, because she could quite easily have drawn away before his arms came about her, before his lips met hers.

'Don't be unhappy on your birthday, Jane.' Soft the voice now, and gentle almost. Another dramatic change! She saw his eyes soften to match his voice; her heart was lifted by his sudden smile. 'I'm sorry about what happened out there; it was something for which neither of us can be blamed. ...' A strange inflection edged his tone, a faraway expression entered his eyes. 'You're a very beautiful woman, Jane.'

She stared at him, her mouth moving convulsively, her hands clasped tightly before her, on the table. The candlelight caressed her hair, brought seductive shadows to her face and colour to her eyes. A nerve pulsated in Philippe's throat; she noticed it only because he began to swallow, as if to remove a sudden blockage.

'I don't—don't understand you, Monseigneur,' she whispered. 'You baffle me.'

He inclined his head.

'I can appreciate your feelings,' he said, surprising her yet again. 'But this is your birthday and we're here to celebrate it. The time is now, Jane ... it always is now.'

'With no past and no future,' she murmured, scarcely aware that she spoke at all. Her spirits were lighter because he was not blaming her for what had happened. He obviously ascribed it to the romantic setting in which they found themselves ... although he *had* said she was very lovely ... and tempting. Nevertheless, no harsh blame was directed against her; he was aware of the reason why they were here, that it was his treat for her, to give her pleasure on her birthday, and he was not intending that incident to mar it—not if he could help it. She was grateful to him and as the meal progressed and they chatted as equals, dancing between courses, she found the misery abating until, at the hour of midnight, when he had driven her back to the chateau and they were standing in the hall, she was able to say quite truthfully that it had been a wonderful evening.

'Thank you so very much, Monseigneur, for your kindness in taking me. I had a wonderful birthday altogether.'

'Don't thank me, Jane,' he said quietly, his eyes never leaving her face. 'It was a great pleasure to me as well.'

CHAPTER SIX

SHE slept fitfully, as was to be expected, since her mind was continually on what had occurred earlier, on the moonlit shore of the hotel's private beach. Nothing like that had ever happened to her before. Her love affair with Don had taken a smooth—and perhaps uneventful—course, with no outburts of violent passion on either side. But last evening.... The revelation was still potently alive in her mind—love could be something far more beautiful than anything she had experienced before.

Had Don discovered this fact too?—in his relations with Gina? Yes, Jane felt sure of it, sure he had realised what he was missing in being married to herself. And now she had made a similar discovery, which proved that she and Don had found the wrong partner in each other, for while they were both obviously of a passionate nature, they had never found fulfilment in their sex life together.

The wrong partner.... Her promise to Don would be broken; she would write to him first thing tomorrow, telling him that there was no future for them together, and that he must act in the way he thought best.

That she had fallen in love with her employer she would not at this stage admit, for she did genuinely believe that despite his fascination for her there was time on her part to draw back. She must draw back, simply because Philippe would never want her, a

woman so far beneath him, a woman who was in reality
no more than a servant, and a divorcee in addition.

Her intention of writing to Don was delayed owing
to Tamsin's being off-colour. Philippe sent for the
doctor, who said it was some childish indisposition that
was not serious, but he prescribed a day or two in bed.
The child was fretful, and another revelation to Jane
was the infinite patience shown by Philippe, who stayed
with Tamsin for a whole afternoon because she had
asked him to sit by the bed and read to her. Jane,
watching from the door, knew a quickening of a pulse,
a yearning for something that was not physical, but
spiritual and mental. Philippe was a real gem, a man
in a million.

Meri had spoken to Jane a few days previously, saying it was rumoured that, now the children had become
orphans, with no one but their uncle to take care of
them, Yvette was not willing to marry him.

'She does not like children at all,' added Meri. 'If
she did marry Monseigneur then she would dislike
very much to have children.'

Jane had naturally dwelt on what she had been told,
wondering if Yvette had decided that marriage without love would be unbearable. Another thing which
came to Jane's mind was her own doubts about Mr
Scott's being dead. She was almost sure Philippe had
lied—but why?

The explanation was to come to her later, but for
the present she was so puzzled that she wished she
had the temerity to broach the subject to her employer.

As it happened the whole mystery was to be cleared
up sooner than she expected.

She had wandered into the garden as usual, after

eating her dinner in her sitting-room, and within minutes a sound penetrated the quietness, and the dark silhouette of Philippe could be seen against the crystal spray of the illuminated fountain. Jane caught her breath. So tall and distinguished, so potently masculine! Vibrations shook her, causing her to blush because of what they meant. This same situation had occurred last evening when, after dining alone, Philippe had decided to take a stroll in the cool of the evening. He and Jane had met and walked together ... and she had come out tonight in the hope that she would meet him again, in the romantic atmosphere of the tropical, night-scented grounds of the chateau where flowers abounded—jasmine sweeping over a wall to mingle with the purple bougainvillaea vine that rioted up from the opposite side; trailing white and pink geraniums, mimosas waving against a backcloth of shrubs.

The anticipation of a few moments with him caused her to quicken her steps, caused her pulse to race, her mind to register the fact that she had in the last few days suddenly come to life. There was magic all around and magic in her heart, erasing the awareness that she belonged to another man, was tied to him until he or she did something about it.

Last night Philippe had been rather aloof, yet friendly in that he chatted with her, mainly about the children. And he took her arm at one point in their stroll, when they were in deep shadow where the terrace rose above the path they were on. The contact had affected her profoundly, but she was guarded, determined not to encourage him ... although the effort was agonisingly difficult. But tonight was different, she was again in a reckless mood, her senses defying control.

She was excited, eager for something to happen regardless of the consequences.

'So we meet again,' was his greeting as he came up to her, his manner relaxed in some strange, unfathomable way that sent a thrill of anticipation rippling through her body. No explanation came to her; all she knew was that the feeling could be the prelude to something indescribably pleasant.

'Yes, Monseigneur. I—I felt like a stroll. The night is so beautiful, and balmy....' Shyness overcame her and she heard him laugh softly before he spoke.

'You're a romantic, Jane. Why aren't you married? Are all Englishmen blind that they haven't seen the beauty both without and within?'

They had come to a halt by the fountain. Jane averted her head, aware that her expression revealed guilt. She had no wish for him to discern that guilt, helped by the lights which so subtly lit the clear crystal waters.

'This garden, this whole island, is romantic, Monseigneur,' she managed at length, deliberately bypassing all but his first sentence.

He seemed to lapse into thought and presently she was emboldened to lift her eyes. She saw the firm strong profile whose contours were highlighted by moonglow, was vitally conscious of his magnetism, the draw of his personality, the fascination of his looks, the thrilling awareness of muscles of steel within his lean lithe frame....'

She looked away again, and as the silence stretched, broken only by the waters of the Indian Ocean cascading over the reef into the lagoon, the truth was upon her, admitted quietly, resignedly, into her consciousness.

She was in love with this noble Frenchman for whom she worked ... irrevocably, and hopelessly, in love.

The silence between them continued and she stared unseeingly at the dark outline of the distant join between sky and sea. Somewhere beyond the horizon was her husband, the man who was waiting patiently for her to go back to him. It would be better if she went—and there was nothing to prevent her because she had not yet written the letter which a few days ago she had resolved to write. Yes, better to return, take up some sort of life and have an aim, a future. For there was no future here, loving a man who could never love her.

He glanced down and she coloured delicately, the blood quickening in her veins. The night was too hauntingly beautiful and romantic ... a night for lovers, for the exchange of tender words and kisses, of rapture indescribable. The moment suddenly became tense, with Philippe's mood incomprehensible, disquieting. While for herself—Jane had the sensation of being suspended in an emotional vacuum, far from the realities of life. Philippe spoke, as if he had to cut the silence. His prosaic words broke the spell and for Jane there was a moment of chill in the atmosphere.

'You seem to have settled here without the slightest difficulty, Jane.'

'It was the children,' she replied. 'I was concerned about them.' She stopped, frowning. Why was she saying this? He knew why she was here, and why she had chosen to stay. Yet she carried on, saying that Barry and Tamsin had become important in her life, that it was as if they and she had been brought together for some reason or purpose. Her voice sank as she ended, because she was a little puzzled by her own words, not quite knowing what she had meant to convey. Philippe seemed to give a slight start before replying,

'Some reason or purpose. A strange thing to say, Jane, and yet.... There could be some truth in it.' His gaze was far away, his body so close that she would only have to move a hand to touch it.

'I don't understand, Monseigneur.' A quiver of air stirred her hair and she put up a hand automatically to remove a tendril from her forehead.

'Fate, my dear,' replied Philippe softly. 'It is the most unpredictable thing in our lives.' A moment's pause and then he quoted, ' "It takes two of us to discover truth: one to utter it and one to understand it." '

Jane's lovely eyes were wide with bewilderment.

'I still don't understand you, Monseigneur.'

'You will, quite soon.'

'Soon? Why not now?' she asked, an unconscious note of petulance in her voice that attracted his attention and brought a lift of censure to his straight dark eyebrows.

She said hastily, before he could admonish her,

'You speak so strangely. You have me extremely puzzled, Monseigneur.'

Faintly he smiled.

'It is natural,' he conceded. 'I speak to you in riddles.'

Encouraged by his tone, she ventured to mention what had been puzzling her.

'The children's father—you said he was dead.' She watched him alertly as she spoke, saw the closed ex-

pression on his face. He began to walk towards the
chateau and she followed, but he stopped suddenly
and she knew instinctively that he was going to say
something of vital importance. But Jane, right behind
him, failed to stop in time and before she knew it she
was against his body, his strong arms reaching out to
steady her.

'Sorry,' he said. 'I oughtn't to have stopped so suddenly.' His grey eyes lit with ardour; his hands remained on her arms. She felt her heart hammering
almost painfully, experienced a thrill of sheer ecstasy
at his touch and the contact of his hard and virile body
temptingly pressed to hers. Her face lifted to his, the
expression in her eyes innocently provocative, seductively tempting. Her temples began to throb as stirrings
of desire shook her from head to foot, and when
Philippe slowly bent his head she waited, in a spell of
eager anticipation which took her very breath away,
for the kiss she knew was to come.

And for a long, long moment they were both lost
in the realm of sensual pleasure. His hand caught and
held one small firm breast, crushing it possessively
while his mouth explored her lips and throat and the
alluring curves that were hidden by the thin lacy
material of her blouse. When at last he released her
she was fighting for breath, because his arms were
like hawsers of steel, closing in with the rapid increase
of his passion.

'Oh. . . .' Nothing more as she gulped, drawing air
deeply into her lungs.

'You're so . . . beautiful! I never thought——' He
broke off abruptly and his whole manner changed,
staggering her as he pulled further away, withdraw-

ing his hands. He waited until she had managed to collect herself before he spoke, resuming what was broached by Jane before the passionate interlude. 'You mentioned the children's father. There was a reason, obviously.' His gaze in the glow from the hidden lamps was anxious, she thought, uncertain.

She paused, searching vainly for tactful words.

'I'm not convinced he's dead,' she told him at last with a hint of apology.

'What makes you think he isn't dead?'

'I've a friend who writes to me—Nora—and she's in constant touch with Mrs Davis, the lady you corresponded with. She's never mentioned anything to Nora about Mr Scott's being dead. In fact, Nora said in her last letter that they—the English police—were still searching for him.'

'I see....' He looked thoughtfully at her. 'You're of the opinion that I lied when I said he was dead?'

'Monseigneur,' said Jane, distressed, 'you put me in a very awkward position.'

'Yes,' he agreed, surprising her, 'I'm aware of it.'

'It would be a strange coincidence indeed if the children's father were dead, so soon after the death of their mother.' She was uncomfortable and looked it. She owed him respect, but for all that she found herself adding, 'Yes, Monseigneur, I do think that you were not quite truthful when you said that Mr Scott was dead.' Would she be enlightened, or reprimanded? She looked at him anxiously, saw the slight lift of his brows as he said,

'Not *quite* truthful? Most diplomatic, Jane.'

She coloured and glanced down.

'You had a good reason, obviously?'

'A very good reason, Jane.' Something in his tone caught at her nerves, alerting them.

'Yes, Monseigneur?'

A pause, slight but tense.

'I wanted Miss Sutcliffe to believe that the children would be with me for ever—well, at least for many years to come.' He spoke calmly as if, now that he had committed himself, he had no reason for hesitancy.

She stared. Such a simple explanation after all! Why had it not occurred to her? She knew too the reason why he had Yvette at the chateau for the fortnight; it was to let her have a taste of what life would be like if she married him. The children would be there the whole time.

'Miss Sutcliffe doesn't like children——' Jane stopped, putting a hand to her mouth. She ought not to have said a thing like that. However, Philippe was nodding, and when he spoke there was a harsh, steely edge to his tone.

'She was to have married me.' He paused a second before continuing, telling Jane all that she knew already, having learned it from Meri. 'I intended to marry her at first because a promise like that is not to be broken. However, I realised that she and I weren't suited, not in any way at all——' Again he stopped and this time his eyes became fixed on Jane's face, a face that was pale and a trifle drawn, the result of his lovemaking and her own resultant despair that it meant nothing to him, nothing more than a diversion, pleasant but trivial. 'I suppose,' he resumed slowly as if speaking to himself, 'that I began to discover that married life could hold something deeper than she or I could give to one another.'

'But you couldn't actually tell her,' put in Jane perceptively. Why was he confiding in her? Where was the air of superiority, the arrogant attitude that was so much a part of him as to be almost always present?

'No, that was not possible. I wanted *her* to break off the affair, which she has done.'

'Because of the children?'

'Exactly, because of the children.'

'Because she believes they're to be here always?'

'Right again.' There was a ruthless quality about him that made Jane say,

'You deliberately brought about a situation in which Miss Sutcliffe would play right into your hands, breaking off your association and freeing you from the promise you had made....' She trailed off, colour fluctuating in her cheeks. 'I'm sorry, Monseigneur. It's none of my business.'

'I have made it your business,' he returned with firm deliberation, and she stared at him uncomprehendingly.

'My business? But how——? I don't see how, Monseigneur.'

'You will presently,' he assured her with the same deliberation. 'I admit I set out to effect the break although, as I have said, in the beginning I had no intention of breaking the promise I'd made to a dying man.'

'No, I understand,' said Jane.

'At that time I liked Miss Sutcliffe and believed we could get along tolerably well. It came as a complete surprise to me to learn of her aversion to children. Naturally I expected an heir, but realised that she would have been most reluctant to have a child.' He

paused, because Jane was blushing at his confidences.
But a moment later he was speaking again, coldly, without a trace of emotion, and Jane learned to her astonish-
ment that he had heard from the British authorities
that Mr Scott was known to be alive and would be
located in the near future. 'But that is the limit of my
knowledge,' he added when Jane would have interrupted him to learn more. 'So you see, my position
would be the same as before once he was found and
was willing to take his children off my hands.'

Jane was still bewildered by his confidences; she had
still been given no clue as to where she came into the
picture.

'Mr Scott might not want the children,' was all she
could find to say.

'I believe he will,' stated Philippe. 'I've talked to
the children and undoubtedly there was a strong bond
between them and their father—a much stronger one
than between them and their mother. It would appear
that Mr Scott's action in deserting his family was because of his continued disagreements with his wife.'

'It's believed that he went off with someone else.
My friend mentioned it in one of her recent letters.'

'That is something I do not know about.'

'You said—said that this business concerns—me,'
she said, casting him a questioning look.

'I must safeguard the freedom which Miss Sutcliffe
has given me ... and the only way to do it is to become engaged to another woman before Mr Scott turns
up.'

Jane stared, her throat going dry, her heartbeats
quickening.

'Oh ... I see....'

A small silence ensued before he said,

'I believe you do, Jane. If I am engaged when the children leave me, then Miss Sutcliffe can have no claim on me whatsoever, simply because it was by her choosing that she and I severed our relationship.'

'Yes,' murmured Jane feverishly, 'and so . . .?'

'I am asking you to do me the favour of becoming my fiancée——'

'No!' She shook her head vigorously. She had guessed what he intended—indeed she would have been little short of stupid if she had not—but to hear it spoken, and in such bland conventional tones, just as if he had been requesting her to do some small and insignificant service for him. 'No, it's impossible! You see, I'm m——'

'Why is it impossible, Jane?' His voice was suddenly tinged with hardness. 'You received letters which are in a man's handwriting, but you're obviously not engaged—if you were you'd not be here, would you?'

Jane nodded automatically.

'No—I'm n-not engaged.'

'Then what is the obstacle?'

'Only the small matter of my marriage,' she wanted to say, but some force beyond her control held back the words, as if affording her a respite in which to give the matter more consideration.

'It will be a temporary arrangement,' he said when she made no answer, 'and I shall make it worth your while.'

She flung out her hands in a negative gesture.

'It isn't possible!' she cried. 'Oh, Monseigneur, you don't understand!'

'I've asked you why it isn't possible.'

She looked at him and thought of the admission she had made to herself—that she loved him. If only she were free! To be engaged to him—Stupid mind-wanderings! What difference would it make if she were free? Philippe did not want her; she was to be a pawn in his game against Yvette, to be used to his advantage and then cast aside.

No, she would not be used!

Philippe repeated his question yet again. She tried to answer, to confess that she was married ... but if she did he would naturally ask for details and as she related them he would learn that she no longer loved her husband and therefore he would naturally consider that she had no valid reason for refusing to help him in his dilemma. And the more she thought about it the more she felt she would have to agree: there really was no valid reason why she should refuse to help him. And she had to admit that his cause was a fair and reasonable one. The promise had become a burden and Yvette, aware of this, should have released him long before now.

'If—If I agree, what will happen—if and when Mr Scott takes the children?'

'We shall remain engaged for a time and then break it off by mutual agreement.'

He had it all worked out to perfection, she thought, but found herself saying, as the idea came to her.

'When we part—you and I—Miss Sutcliffe might consider the situation between you and her to be the same as before.'

Philippe was already shaking his head.

'She has made the choice; she can't expect me to marry her after she's refused. No, she won't trouble me again—not after we announce our engagement.' He smiled, obviously taking her acquiescence for granted. Jane gave a helpless little shrug, her will—as once before—failing under the power of his.

CHAPTER SEVEN

ABSENTLY Jane twisted the ring on her finger, the letter she had received that morning there in front of her on the dressing-table, her thoughts jostling between its contents and the role she had agreed to play.

Don had begun the letter by saying how lonely he was, that the house was dead without her, that there was nothing in his life and never would be until she came back to him. And then he had continued,

'I didn't take my annual holiday, because there was nothing I could do on my own. But now the idea has come to me that I could have a fortnight in Mauritius and we could be together during your free time. I promise not to embarrass you in any way, darling, by making myself known. I'll be your brother if you like but I see no reason why I couldn't come as a friend, do you?'

When she had first taken in the contents of his letter Jane had been on the verge of panic, but with the passing of a few hours she had managed to regain her calm, to observe the situation objectively, and to determine the course she must take. It was simple: she would tell her husband that everything was over, that he could go ahead and get a divorce. She realised now that she should have written before, at the time the resolution came to her, but having put it off on account of Tamsin's illness, she had never got down to doing it. Well, she would do it now, she decided.

But that was half an hour ago, before she had noticed the postscript which had been written on the back of the single sheet of paper. The paper had been folded in three, and the postscript written on the middle space, so that it was not obvious either when Jane unfolded the sheet, or folded it again. She had slipped it into the envelope and it was only when she had taken it out again, after seeing the children safely in the car with Bhoosan, that the postscript had caught her eye.

'I *shall come*, Jane even though you try to put me off. I'm determined to see you, and am going out today to book my flight.'

The letter was dated just over a week ago....

What must she do? Don would have to be told of her decision, and she hoped he would then go away— take a holiday at one of the hotels and then go home again. It sounded all right—no real complications. Sounded.... Because she was trying to convince herself, trying to ward off the kind of near-panic that had assailed her when she had first received the letter and taken in its contents.

It *wasn't* all right. Obviously Don had suddenly had a suspicion that she would try to put him off, so he had added the postscript. And not only that, but he had gone off and booked his flight. There was a threat in his words, she believed. She knew him, had had experience of his determination and tenacity once he had made up his mind about anything; his refusal to listen to Jane's plea when she had wanted him to give Gina up was proof of that. He would come whatever she said—— In fact, he could already be in Mauritius....

What of Philippe's reaction if he learned the truth—

that she was married and had deliberately lied to him?
And what of Don's reaction on discovering that his
wife had become engaged to another man?

'God, what a muddle! Why did I agree to get engaged to Philippe?'

She thrust the letter away, out of sight in a drawer,
and went on to the balcony. Peace was here, in the
lovely grounds of the chateau. Reality was a million
miles away and she meant to remember that, at least
for a few minutes or so. She sat down on a rattan chair
and tried to relax. But she was restless and she soon got
up and went into the grounds, following a path
bordered by flower beds, and where in a little arbour
was a rustic seat. She occupied this for several minutes
before springing to her feet again. Supposing Don was
here, and was already on his way to the chateau? She
felt instinctively, with every moment that passed, that
he would cause trouble for her. She would lose her
job, and the esteem of her employer ... her fiancé....
She looked upon him as her fiancé, partly because he
had instructed her to act as if she were in love with
him—because although Yvette had broken with him
she still visited the chateau once or twice a week—and
partly because she *wanted* to act as if they were really
engaged. It was a daydream that was stupid, but she
indulged in it. She loved him, so it was easy to live
the part. One day her dream would fade to nothing
but a memory, but for the present is was very real to
Jane and the last thing she wanted was for her husband
to come here and reveal his identity to Philippe.

She paced the lawn, then went back into the house.
Meri met her in the hall and said that Miss Sutcliffe
had called and was in the living-room. This was a cosy

apartment which lacked any formality at all; it was for the family, not for visitors or guests, even those who were intimate friends of Philippe.

'Monseigneur is not in and I wondered if you would like to keep Miss Sutcliffe company.' There was deep respect in Meri's attitude these days, since the engagement. It had been a nine days' wonder to everyone at the chateau when it was announced, and already Jane was being tentatively asked when the wedding was going to be. Philippe had told her to say that it would not be for about six months or so.

'By that time the children should be back with their father,' he had continued, 'and our engagement can be broken without its appearing ever to have been a put-up job.' He was frowning as he spoke of the break and she wondered if the idea was abhorrent to him. She imagined it would be, since he was not the kind of man to make a mistake like that in the first place.

'I'll go and see Miss Sutcliffe, Meri. Will you bring in some coffee and biscuits in about five or ten minutes, please?'

'Certainly, mademoiselle,' returned Meri with a smile.

Yvette was lounging on a velvet-covered settee, her back against the cushions, one shapely leg outstretched along the seat. It was a pose that irritated Jane, but one that the girl invariably adopted, though never in Philippe's presence. She had taken the news of the engagement almost uninterestedly, on the surface, but Jane always sensed a deep hatred smouldering within the girl and she sometimes felt that Yvette would do her an injury if ever the chance should come her way.

'Good morning, Miss Sutcliffe.' Jane's voice was low, cool and polite. 'You wanted to see Philippe?'

Yvette seemed to wince at Jane's easy use of Philippe's name, but she immediately produced a smile as she replied,

'I have some records of his, but I've forgotten what they are. I felt I had better return them. I expect he's got a list.

'He isn't in; Meri told you.'

Yvette nodded her head, her dark eyes roving Jane's figure insolently.

'You look very happy,' she remarked, her glance darting to Jane's face. 'You've fallen on your feet, becoming engaged to a man as wealthy as Philippe.'

Jane gasped, as well she might, and a thread of crimson creeping along the sides of her mouth gave evidence of the anger rising within her.

'You put it rather crudely,' she said, trying to keep the anger from her voice. 'I'm fortunate, yes, but I don't think Philippe would be pleased to hear you say I've fallen on my feet.'

'He's a strange man,' musingly as with languid grace Yvette reached for her handbag and opened it. 'He acts impulsively at times. Not a good trait, impulsiveness.'

'You're implying that his action in asking me to—to become engaged to him was impulsive?' Somehow, she had never been able to mention marriage to anyone, simply because there wasn't to be a marriage.

'He wanted a mother for those children, and you were the obvious choice because you happened to be here.'

Jane could have allowed her anger to break the

reins if it hadn't been for the thread of amusement
that wove through it, bringing an involuntary smile
to her lips. The girl believed she had it all sorted out—
but how very mistaken she was!

'I happen to like the children,' she said, still amused
'and that's important.' She looked significantly at her
but this either escaped Yvette's notice or she chose t
ignore it.

'You admit, then, that Philippe is marrying you
merely for the children's sake?'

'I don't remember having admitted anything of th
sort.'

'It's true, nevertheless, and you know it!' Yvett
had taken out a cigarette and the gold case was sud
denly snapped shut. 'You'll both regret it!'

Jane looked at her, wondering why pity should nov
be her chief emotion. Yet the girl did need pity; sh
was suffering bitter disappointment, since she had be
lieved she would marry Philippe, and even thoug
she knew he had no love for her, the ambition to b
his wife had remained. It must be sheer misery to si
and talk with the woman who was taking your place
And at the thought Jane's face shadowed. She hersel
would be replaced one day; but thank heaven she woul
never meet the woman who would capture Philippe'
heart.

His heart *would* be captured; Jane had no doub
about that whatsoever.

Meri appeared with the tray, appearing to be
trifle uncomfortable as she put it down on a low antiqu
table, avoiding Yvette's eyes.

'Will there be anything else, mademoiselle?' sh
enquired of Jane.

'No, thank you, Meri.'

'Shall I pour the coffee?' she asked, but Jane, aware that the Creole girl was embarrassed at having to give most of her respect to the girl who she believed would one day become her mistress, said no, she would pour the coffee herself.

This she did, pouring it from a silver pot, watched narrowly by the girl on the couch.

'Will you come to the table?' invited Jane in a dignified tone. She was aware that Yvette wanted her to comment on what she had said, but Jane was determined to ignore it. However, some compulsion seemed to force Yvette to repeat it, and this time her voice was not only high-pitched, but virulent.

'I said you'll both regret it!' Yvette flicked a lighter and touched the end of her cigarette. 'I never thought Philippe could be so rash as to marry purely in order to get someone to take care of the children—children who aren't even related to him——!' She broke off, drawing a breath as the door opened to admit the man she had been talking about. 'You!' she faltered. 'I——I——'

'So you consider me rash, do you, Yvette?' The cold, steely voice was like a rasp. 'Jane dear, I can only apologise to you on Yvette's behalf because it is doubtful if she will apologise for herself.'

Jane shivered at his tone, hoping she herself never had his anger directed against her. His eyes, too, were flecked with glittering points of steel and his mouth was tightly compressed. Jane had felt sorry for Yvette before; she felt even more sorry for her now as, rising from the settee, she gathered up her handbag and gloves and stalked towards the door, trying desperately to assume a dignified air but failing miserably.

Philippe turned his attention to Jane when the door had closed—or rather, slammed—behind the other girl. In spite of the apology he had made his whole manner was stern, admonishing.

'You should have retaliated, Jane,' he told her severely. 'You don't allow anyone to speak to you like that—*anyone*, understand?'

'Y-yes, Philippe.' She was staring dazedly at him, staggered by his censure and the imperious way it was delivered. He might almost be her *real* fiancé! 'It—it w-was awkward. . . .'

'Remember your dignity, and the respect due to you as my betrothed,' he said sternly. 'I shall expect you in future to put Yvette in her place.' He paused, but Jane had nothing at all to say. She was close to tears, smarting under his reprimand, which she felt was unkind, seeing that he knew what she had endured from Yvette. 'I didn't hear much, but enough to arouse my anger. What else had she to say?'

Jane looked hard at him, blinking quickly as she replied,

'She believes you've become engaged to me because you want a mother for Barry and Tamsin.'

'She does?' The anger dissolved, replaced by a hint of amusement in the curve of his lips. 'Well, well . . . it has its funny side, hasn't it?'

She swallowed, nodding her head. The mistiness of her eyes caught his attention and he frowned.

'I suppose so,' she answered flatly.

Philippe was standing with his back to the high wide fireplace, a tall erect figure immaculate in faultless grey slacks and a blouson type jacket with suede pockets. Jane looked at him, wishing he did not always appear so attractive to her. She was endeavouring to control her emotions regarding him, aware as she was that heartache was shortly to be hers. If she could only stop loving him, or at least love him a little less ... and less ... and less until she reached a point where the agony of parting would not be so great. How did one stop loving a man? She had stopped loving her husband—but then he had not treated her right, had betrayed her, broken the vows he had so eagerly made.

'Jane....' Philippe's voice was gentle, and he was moving quietly towards her, his hands reaching out to her. 'You're almost crying.' His eyes were dark with regret. 'Was I too stern with you? Perhaps I should not have been quite so angry.' His hands reached down now and Jane was drawn to her feet. Tremblingly she looked at him, the tears even closer because of his gentleness, his concern for her. 'My child....' His fingers stroked her hair, gently, then came down to her face to flick away the first tear to fall. 'I'm sorry, Jane dear. I expect it was my pride that was affected——'

'But we're not really engaged,' she reminded him, her voice catching as a tiny sob rose in her throat. 'So why was your pride injured?'

'Because Yvette believes we're engaged,' he answered. 'And in that case you, as my fiancée, would be expected to put her in her place if she insults you.'

'You mean, Philippe, that if I don't—er—put her in her place, she might begin to suspect something?'

'Exactly.' His eyes softened. 'It's difficult for you, I know, but you will try to please me by adopting the dignity which would be expected of my—wife.' Before she had time to say anything he had bent his

head and she felt the tender pressure of his mouth
on her softly parted lips. 'And now, what about this
coffee? It'll be getting cold.' He drew away, glancing
at the two cups of coffee which Jane had already poured
out. 'It *is* cold,' he declared without touching either
of the cups. 'I'll ring for Meri to bring us some more.'

There followed a pleasant, companionable interlude
with neither of them speaking, each busy with their
own thoughts. Jane naturally dwelt on the little scene
that had followed Philippe's angry one—his tenderness towards her, his apology for making her cry. But
what forced itself to the forefront of her mind was the
way he had said '... my—wife.'

There had been no need to use that word at all,
and certainly no need to say it with that particular intonation, as if there had been a tender thought within
him as he spoke. Was she being fanciful? Several times
she had wondered if he liked her in *that* kind of way.
A sigh that was almost an exclamation escaped her and
he glanced towards her across the low table at which
they were sitting. His eyes questioning, but she merely
laughed and said lightly that her coffee had gone down
the wrong way. What if he was beginning to like her?
Jane's musings were resumed and again her breath
caught but this time silently, controlled. It would never
do for Philippe to fall in love with her and want to
marry her. It would be terrible because of her deceit,
and even if he forgave her the deceit there was still
the obstacle of her marriage.

Sheer misery swept through her in a tide of despair
and hopelessness. Philippe would never forgive her
nor would he ever consider marrying a woman who had

been through the divorce court. She was as sure of that as she was of sitting here.

Her mind switched to Don, who was probably on his way to Mauritius, or even already here. Another complication in her life, and as if that weren't enough Philippe told her, the following morning, that he had heard from England and was assured that Mr Scott was willing to take his children. He could not come over for another six weeks, but he certainly would be there, and he would take his children away with him when he left.

Sheer dismay enveloped Jane; she felt overwhelmed by anxiety at the thought of another upheaval for them. They were so happy and settled; they were doing well at school. They adored Meri and Rima; Bhoosan was their friend. They got on with their uncle, and they loved their nanny.

And now they were to be taken away . . . to where?

Philippe did not know any more than he had told her. He was expecting to have a letter from Mr Scott, but until it arrived he did not know where he was intending to take Barry and Tamsin.

Jane's knowledge naturally affected her manner with the children and the following day she was fussing over them, petting them, allowing them all their own way. It was Saturday and they spent the entire morning and most of the afternoon on the beach, making castles and knocking them down again. They went in the sea romped along the sands, had tea on the lawn beneath the shade of a takamaka tree, and after she had put them to bed she read to them. She was in a state of almost feverish unhappiness, with the future bleak, both for the children and for herself.

At dinner that evening Philippe noticed her pallor and her silence and quite naturally remarked on them. She tried to throw off her dejection but failed, and eventually was forced to tell Philippe the reason for her unhappiness—or one of the reasons.

'It's Barry and Tamsin, Philippe. Are they going to adjust, after the lovely life they're having here?'

'They'll have to, Jane,' he answered. 'I am not intending to keep them permanently, even if their father would agree, which I feel sure he would not. You know the reason for my agreeing to take them—because I wanted to test Yvette. They're not really related to me, so I do not think I have a duty towards them.'

'No, I do understand, Philippe.'

Should she confess all—throw herself on Philippe's mercy? His anger would be terrible to see, for not only would he learn of her deceit, but he would realise that he had given his love to a woman who was bound to another man. Total disillusionment. . . . No! Jane could not bear to see him hurt and bitter, hating her, despising himself. Again she wondered what was to be the end of it. She looked at Philippe across the candlelit table. He was anxious about her, she knew, and forced a smile to her lips.

'I'm sorry to be miserable, Philippe. I've grown to love the children, you see—just as you have.' She paused and her eyes became luminous as one of the candles hissed, and the flame shot up. 'I do realise that their place is with their father, but. . . .' She trailed away, not really knowing what she wanted to say.

'You're not miserable, dear, just unhappy. And I hate to see you like this.' His hand reached out across the table, to cover hers. Warmth suffused her body and this time when she smiled it was spontaneous, a happy smile. She thought: take what is offered for as long as you can. Gather memories; they're to last you all your life.

Yes, all her life for there could never be anyone else.

Later, when the meal was over and they had had their coffee on the terrace, Philippe took Jane's arm possessively as they strolled through gardens spangled with moonlight, on to the beach. The night was silent but for the rush of water over the reef; the lagoon was a mirror painted with silver by the moon's lambent glow. From the deep purple dome of the heavens a million points of argent light flickered and twinkled—diamonds in a bed of velvet. A gentle breeze swayed the palms and the casuarinas along the shore, while just beyond, in the woods, light and shadow wove a tapestry of lace.

Jane gave a deep sigh of contentment. She was determined to live for the present, uncaring of both past and future. The time was now, it always was, Philippe had said, and how very true! Today you were alive; tomorrow was unpredictable.

'What was that for?' Philippe slowed his pace, glancing into her upturned face, an inscrutable expression on his.

'The beauty——' She spread a hand expressively, drawing an imaginary half-cirle. 'I never thought, a few months ago, that I'd ever see anything like this.' Lacy clouds of cobweb silk were curling into the sky, creating a silver haze over the lagoon so that it seemed even more placid than before, unmoving except for where the reef lay, enclosing the translucent waters

that gently caressed the pure white sand of the shore.
'No wonder Mark Twain said heaven was fashioned
on Mauritius.'

Philippe listened in silence, his grey eyes never leaving her face. It was a tense and tender moment, with
every nerve in Jane's body taut, her beautiful eyes
seeking enlightenment. She felt sure he loved her, but
she wanted to hear it from his lips. And yet, in spite of
her desire, there was a hollowness within her, knowing
as she did that nothing could come of their love for
one another.

The words did not come; instead, he bent his head
to take her lips in a long and tender kiss. She clung
to him, silently revealing her love while at the same
time half relieved that he had not told her of his.
It would be better if he did not love her, she thought,
for then his disillusionment, his bitter disappointment
in her would not go so deep.

'My dear, dear Jane....' His lips left hers just long
enough for the tender words to be spoken. 'I want
you——' His words were cut by the appearance of
someone else coming along the shore.

Jane sighed for the moment that was lost, and a wistful shadow lay in the soft brown eyes that were raised
to his. It was only when Philippe said,

'Who the devil can this be?' that she remembered
this was his private beach and that no other person
should be using it.

She looked, then—and her heart seemed to leap
right into her throat. That walk ... she would know
it anywhere!

She wanted to turn and run, but her legs were like

jelly. Prepared as she was for the appearance of her husband, Jane had never visualised him coming to the chateau, much less coming out to look for her. In a flash she knew what had occurred: he had gone to the house and had been told by Meri that Mademoiselle had gone walking with Monseigneur. Further than this Jane refused to theorise. The fact of Don's coming to look for her was enlightenment enough of the mood he would be in. Had he seen her and Philippe in that intimate pose? Undoubtedly he had, since they were clearly silhouetted in the moonlight, two people as one, so close were their bodies to each other.

She spoke swiftly, amazed that words were articulated at all, for the blockage in her throat made speech exceedingly difficult.

'It's—it's a—a friend of m-mine, Philippe,' she stammered. 'He—er—wrote to s-say he would be coming for a holiday, and—and he's here.' She ended on a lame and almost inaudible note, her eyes downcast, her small hands clasped together in front of her. She was vaguely conscious of such things as Philippe's incredulous little gasp, of the hem of her evening gown getting somehow under her sandal, of the dark figure hurrying towards them ... shortening the distance with frightening speed.

'You were expecting a visitor—a *man* visitor—and never told me?' The words were slow but emphasised and faintly harsh. 'I find that astounding.' No response from Jane and he added tautly, 'Am I to understand that this is the man who writes to you so regularly?'

'Yes, it—it is,' she nodded, lifting her face as Don came up to them at last.

'So you're here!' Fury caused his voice to vibrate, and again Jane spoke urgently, adopting an attitude of lightness—and welcome.

'Don! I didn't expect you yet! I mean, I thought you'd be staying at a hotel and would contact me from there! It's—n-nice to see you! You're looking well—— Oh, I'm sorry—let me introduce you to—to my employer, Monsieur de Chameral. Monseigneur—Mr Donald——' Her voice hung suspended while her heartbeats raced, thudding like hammers in her chest. She wondered how she could ever have loved Don, as at this moment she hated him with a black venom.

'Yes?' prompted Philippe softly.

'My name's Clark,' snapped Don, 'the same as hers!'

Philippe's eyes flickered from one face to the other.

'You're related?'

'Distantly,' interposed Jane in desperation, her eyes pleading with her husband, but at the same time she hoped they conveyed the warning that any denunciation would do him more harm than good. She wanted to frighten him into silence just to give herself a re-spite—time to think, and to make her confession to Philippe in her own way. She waited, taut and breathless, for him to speak, and when he did her whole body sagged with relief.

'Yes, very distantly.'

'I see.' So soft the tone but cold and colourless. Jane could have wept, but instead she managed a light laugh as she said,

'It's so distant that we're only friends, really, aren't we, Don?'

He answered her through lips that scarcely opened.

'Yes, we're merely friends.'

'Of long standing?' enquired Philippe, still in that same colourless tone.

'Several years,' replied Don tightly.

Philippe's inscrutable eyes flickered from Don's face to Jane's, then back again.

'You've obviously been up to the house?'

Don nodded briefly.

'I have, and was told that Jane was somewhere out here.' His manner was belligerent and Jane, catching his eye, gave him another warning look. She was angry and in a mood to turn on him. She wished that Philippe were not here. Don's attitude changed as he accepted her warning. A smile came to his lips as he added, 'I thought I'd come out and see if I could find her. I hope you don't mind, Monsieur de Chameral?'

'Not at all.'

'It was impulsive of me, I know, but it was disappointing not to find Jane in, so I came out here.' He seemed to be losing confidence altogether, noticed Jane with a sort of spiteful satisfaction.

'You hadn't informed Jane as to the time you would be arriving?' Philippe's straight dark brows had lifted fractionally. Jane, noticing the colour creeping into her husband's cheeks, noticed also that her satisfaction had increased.

'It was very remiss of me,' he admitted sulkily, his eyes lowered as if he was unable to meet the piercing regard of the distinguished Frenchman who had been kissing his wife. Looking from one to the other, Jane found herself comparing them—their height and physique, their looks, their manner, and she suddenly knew a sort of reluctant contempt for her husband. He was put out by the sheer magnificence of Philippe; she felt sure that if he were to speak at this moment he would be stammering like a schoolboy who was totally unsure of himself.

Philippe said, his glance flicking Jane's face,

'As your friend has just arrived I'll leave you to talk with him. I expect,' he said turning to Don, 'that you're booked in at a hotel?'

'Yes, of course.'

'You have arranged transport back to it?'

'Er—n-no.'

'My car and chauffeur are at your disposal until half-past ten,' he said and, without another glance at Jane, he swung round on his heels and strode away.

CHAPTER EIGHT

'WHAT the hell was he doing kissing you?' The question came almost before Philippe had covered enough distance as to be out of earshot. 'My God, Jane, I don't know how I kept my control?' Sheer fury darkened his eyes and his fists were so tightly clenched that the skin over his knuckles showed white. 'I asked you a question, Jane! I want an answer!'

'Well, you won't get one?' she flashed. 'Instead, I shall ask you a question: what do you mean by coming here——'

'I told you I was coming!'

'I mean here, to the chateau. This is not my house——'

'Are you living with him?' he demanded furiously. 'Are you lovers——?' The resounding slap of Jane's hand against his cheek brought his voice to an amazed halt. He stared disbelievingly, incredulously, at the girl who had always been so loving and gentle.

'You—you struck m-me. Jane, you struck your husband!' He looked ready to cry, she thought, with all the fury and fight gone out of him. 'I never believed you would ever do a thing like that to me.'

'Nor did I ever think you would be unfaithful to me!' she countered. 'How dare you accuse me of living with Philippe! You, who left me to live with that—that—*creature*!—that shameless——'

'Don't say it!'

'Well, she is. . . .' Jane's voice trailed to silence and there was a perceptive pause before she added, slowly, wonderingly, 'You still love her.' It was a statement, so sure was she that she had derived the correct meaning from his vehement exclamation . . . vehement and yet piteous—a cry from the heart.

'No,' he denied, but after a slight pause. 'No! Of course I'm not still in love with her! Would I be here if I were?'

Jane was standing very still, her eyes staring out over the lagoon—a sheet of unmoving water drenched in starlight. So peaceful. . . . And in her heart such turmoil. Her eyes moved to the face of the man who had caused it all and she knew she ought to be pitying him, that in her generosity she should be capable of infinite understanding, and forgiveness. Something terrible and painful caught her throat and she put a quivering hand to it, automatically.

'Don . . . you *do* still love her. . . .'

He turned away and she was staring over his shoulder to the darker places behind the seashore, the mysterious places where night creatures were busy, where orchids grew, and lilies, the quiet places, the gentle landscapes that were born of such terrible thermal unrest so many eons ago.

Unrest was in her heart, and in that of her husband.

For they each loved someone else.

'Don,' she whispered again, and he turned slowly and there were tears in his eyes.

'I don't love her,' he said but weakly. 'It's you I love. Haven't I been telling you in my letters?'

'Telling me untruths,' she stated gently. 'If you still love her, then why don't you try to win her back?'

A great sob shook his body. But he repeated his assertion that he loved his wife, not Gina.

'I want you back——' He stopped, a scowl on his face at the memory of what he had seen when coming along the shore. 'This man you work for. There's more in your relationship with him than employer and employee. He was kissing you.' His eyes raked her figure. 'You said your post was that of nanny to the two children. A nanny doesn't doll herself up like this and let the kids' uncle make love to her.' He stepped back as he spoke as if he half expected to get another slap on his face.

'I dine with Philippe every evening, so I have to wear a long dress——'

'And does dining with him mean that you've to let him kiss you?'

She quivered with sudden anger, unconsciously putting up her left hand to her cheek, because it felt hot.

'You say you want me back, Don, but you might as well know, here and now, that there's no possibility of our taking up where we left off. I don't love you and neither do you love me. Under these circumstances we'd be crazy to get together again, and I really don't know why you want me to come back....' Her voice drifted away to a puzzled silence as she saw his fixed expression, the glassy film across his eyes, giving them an almost frightening look. 'What is it? Are you ill?'

'That—that——' He pointed to her hand, his voice husky and choked. 'It's an engagement ring—not the one I bought y-you.' The fight had gone out of him again and his whole frame seemed to be drooping. 'You *can't* be engaged to him when you're married to me—you *can't*, I say!' His face was ashen in the moonlight; he was trying to convince himself, and failing miserably, as his next words revealed. 'You're in love with him? That's why he was kissing you—because you wanted him to?'

Jane nodded, her anger dissolved by the pity that came at last, sweeping through her mind and leaving her emotionally drained. After all, she had loved him once, had set him high above all other men she knew. Loved him...? She found herself saying reflectively,

'You know, Don, I believe you and I weren't really suited from the start—— Oh, I admit we've been happy, but have we been deliriously so?'

'What do you mean?' She had dropped her hand to her side, but his eyes were still on it, on the beautiful solitaire diamond surrounded by sapphires. 'Of course we were deliriously happy, and could be again.'

But Jane was shaking her head firmly, and yet a little sadly too.

'Be honest,' she begged, 'and admit that you had more from Gina than you ever had from me?'

'No! Oh, Jane, what are you trying to do to me? I want you, only you! I won't give you up to this other man——' He broke off, staring at her for what seemed an eternity. 'He thinks you're single,' he murmured. 'He believes you're free to marry him. Are you crazy? Were you intending to commit bigamy——'

'Don't be absurd,' she flashed, wishing he would not test her temper like this. 'You're talking sheer nonsense and you know it!'

'Then how the devil can you be engaged to him?'

She hesitated, then told him everything, noticing the relaxing of his features as she progressed, until at the end his face was almost serene, so great was his relief. Jane looked frowningly at him and said,

'It doesn't make any difference to us, Don. I've no intention of ever living with you again.' She looked down, moving the soft sand with her foot. 'I want a divorce, Don. I'm very serious about that.'

'So you can marry him?'

'He won't want a divorced woman.'

'Is he in love with you?'

'He was kissing me,' she began, when he interrupted her.

'Doesn't mean a thing! He doesn't seem the kind who would fall in love, anyway, so you're wasting your time in thinking he'll marry you!'

'You're not being very consistent, Don,' she said, 'but it doesn't matter. The only important thing at present is that you and I gain our freedom.'

'There was a time,' he said unpleasantly, 'when you didn't believe in divorce.'

She nodded in agreement, but went on to say,

'It's immoral to live together without love. I know now that, although I hate the idea of divorce, it's the only thing for people like us who've made a mistake.'

'Mistakes can be rectified!'

'Not always—not where relationships like ours are concerned.'

He looked at her, then at the glittering jewels on her finger again.

'What do you mean?'

'That I was quite serious when I said that we were never deliriously happy together, that you had more from Gina than you had from me.'

'Sexually?'

'Yes, that's what I mean.'

His eyes narrowed.

'And you—you can get more from someone else than you did from me?'

She frowned, hesitating.

'It isn't a nice subject, Don,' she said.

'It isn't supposed to be! I've asked you a question!'

'All right, I'll answer you! Yes, I can get more from someone else than I ever had from you!'

'Him?' briefly and with an ugly sneer curling his lips.

'I'm not discussing Philippe with you,' she told him curtly. And then, 'I think it must be nearly half-past ten. You won't be able to have the car if you leave it any longer.'

'I can get a taxi.'

'I'd prefer you to leave now,' she said quietly, half turning from him as an indication of her desire to get away.

'And not come back?'

She swallowed. It was so very sad, she thought. Once they had been lovers and now she never wanted to set eyes on him again.

'There's nothing to be gained by our seeing one another, is there, Don?' Her voice had softened and in her lovely eyes he saw pity. His own eyes brooded and his lip trembled convulsively until he caught it in his teeth, pressing them on to it until it hurt. She said, repeating the question she had asked a few minutes before, 'Why don't you try to win Gina back again, Don? I would, if I were in your place.'

A terrible silence descended and Jane's heart seemed to stop beating for a second as she looked into a face contorted with agony.

'Don ... for God's sake, what———?'

'She's dead—Gina's dead———' To Jane's horror he flung himself face down into the sand at her feet and sobbed till his whole body was a heaving, convulsive shape that looked almost inhuman.

'Dead ... Oh, you poor, poor thing!' She knelt down beside him, her own tears streaming on to his coat. Her arms enclosed him, in a tender protective embrace, gently urging him to turn, and to rise again to his feet.

'I'm sorry—Jane—sorry t-to b-be such a coward, t-taking it so badly.' Taking out a handkerchief, he wiped his eyes, and the sand from his face.

Gently she led him along the shore, into the grounds of the chateau, then to a sheltered arbour where she pushed him down on to a seat.

'How did it happen? Tell me all about it, Don,' she urged softly. 'Everything.'

'She died in hospital three weeks ago———' He put his face in his hands. His shoulders shook and it was some moments before he could continue. 'She was so young to have a heart attack!'

Jane stood there, above his drooping figure, thinking of his emphatic assertion that it was her he loved, when his heart was breaking over the death of the girl he really loved.

'You'd parted,' she reminded him in quiet, gentle tones. 'But it sounds as if there was a making up before she died?'

'Only the week before. I rang her and begged her to meet me and she did. We had a wonderful making up and knew it was for ever.' He stopped to put the handkerchief to his eyes again and Jane said reflectively,

'That would be a month ago. I remember that there was a period that you didn't write—I mean, I usually received a letter every week, sometimes even more often. But about a month ago there was a break. I remember thinking that perhaps you'd suddenly decided that there was no future for you and me and in consequence had thought it best to stop writing.'

He nodded his head, looking up at her with eyes dark and drawn with grief.

'I did intend to write and tell you we'd got together again, and that it was for good so we'd have to have a divorce. But Gina and I decided to go away, to Spain for a week—— It was bliss ... heaven ... nights and days of rapture....' He spoke to himself—a long, long way from the wife who was standing there, listening with pity in her heart but no feeling in the rest of her body. She thought: we go, radiant, to the altar and take our vows, blissfully unaware of the trials that are to beset us in the future. Cynicism, deep and bitter, swept through her. What a fool's paradise young couples live in! But the next moment she was herself again, throwing off such hateful thoughts as she reflected on her love for Philippe ... and his for her. Yes, he loved her; she had seen vicious, burning jealousy look out from those lazy grey eyes just a short while ago. Their love would have endured for ever— if only they had met before, several years ago. Don's voice broke her reverie and she glanced down at him. 'We came back and within two—two d-days she w-was dead, Jane—dead! Oh, God, I don't want to live! Why didn't I go too!'

Jane's heart swelled with compassion, the tears falling unchecked down her face and on to the lovely dress she wore. Automatically Don offered his handkerchief and she took it, discovering it to be soaked.

'I never meant to tell you of her death, Jane, because I wanted you back——'

'You could never live with me, loving her the way you do,' she broke in protestingly.

'I felt it was the only way I'd survive—get over it. All right, I meant to use you, Jane, but I felt sure that eventually we'd be happy again, as we were once, remember?'

She turned from him, wondering why the pity did not shrink and die in her heart. He had meant to use her. . . . He came here with the intention of persuading her to go back to him, to fill a gap, a yawning gap, left by the girl who had died so tragically young.

'It would never have worked,' she said, and her voice was cold, her body still nerveless. 'How could you have believed it would?'

'Because people get over grief in time.'

'But you needed help—my help?' She swung round as she spoke, the bitterness in her mind at variance with the pity in her heart. Don had risen from the seat, his hand reaching out to clutch the skirt of her dress. 'Please leave go——'

'Have pity on me, Jane!' he cried, crushing the dress with frenzied fingers. 'What will I do if you send me away alone? That house——' He shuddered, releasing his hold on the material, then staring at it as if he were wondering how he had come to crease it so much. 'I began to hate the house, the terrible loneliness! Then Gina was back with me again and we went away to——'

'You've told me that,' broke in Jane softly.

'So I have—I don't know what I'm saying! Jane darling, I've only got you——' Before she had time to guess what his fevered mind was planning he had seized her in his arms, arching her backwards so that she was forced to cling to him for support. His head came down and she flinched at the pressure of his mouth on hers.

A shadow brought them apart. Jane, stunned and breathless, heard Philippe's voice—a whiplash in the dark.

'I'm sorry to intrude, but it's almost midnight. I must ask you, Jane, to come in, and you, Mr Clark, to leave!'

'Philippe, please don't think—I mean——' Jane's voice held the desperation of fear, but before she could say any more Don was speaking, in a voice that staggered her by its calm.

'Sorry, Monsieur de Chameral, I forgot the time. Jane, goodnight; I'll telephone you tomorrow morning.'

The following morning Jane awoke to the 'teer, teer, teer', call of the pic-pic, a little bird like a ball of light blue fluff on black legs. It would be on her balcony, and if she went out there it would cock its tiny head to examine her and it might then fly away, but not very far. On other mornings she had delighted in this gentle little creature, and indeed several other birds—the Mauritius parakeet flying past and emitting its familiar 'Hark! Hark!' or the bulbul which came in a small flock to gather fruits and seeds from the woods which formed part of the extensive grounds of the chateau. But this morning she had no enthusiasm for anything, her thoughts when she woke naturally darting to the dramatic incidents of last night. Philippe had been nowhere about when she entered the house, although she had wandered from room to room hoping to find him and to explain. What he would think of her seemed no longer to matter very much. She had never once cherished the idea that he and she would marry, simply because of the barrier which, she knew for sure, was insurmountable. All she wanted was to make her confession, then to explain how she came to be in Don's arms, in what must have appeared to be a passionate embrace. Perhaps in some small degree he would think a little less badly of her when he learned that it had not been her fault in any way at all.

He was absent at the breakfast table and again at lunch time. Don rang at half-past eleven; she had expected the call to be made earlier.

'I must see you,' he had told her urgently. 'I *must*, Jane! You've said in your letters that you're free until the children come from school in the afternoons. I'll meet you in Port Louis.'

'I don't think——'

'If you have any pity, and memories that are worth anything at all, you'll come to me.' Before she could speak he had mentioned the Stag Hotel and then he rang off.

What must she do? The recollection of his action last night was still with her but, strangely enough, her anger was not. She tried to put herself in his place, endeavouring to experience the heartache, the terrible grief and loneliness that he was suffering. She found excuses for most of his intentions and even his actions. He was a man who had to lean on someone—strangely she had never realised this, but then there had never been a situation where he needed someone to lean on, not until now. That he was a weak character had come out most profoundly, but Jane even excused this too, allowing that traits like that were inherent and therefore outside the control of those possessing them.

After a good deal of heart-searching she decided to go and meet him. Bhoosan was at liberty and after making absolutely certain that Philippe would not be requiring the car, she let the chauffeur drive her into the city. He parked just off the main square—the palm-shaded Place d'Armes—and after telling Bhoosan what time she would be back, she went along past Government House and the Municipal Theatre, then along by one of the cathedrals to the Stag Hotel. Don was in the lobby; she saw him before he saw her and frowned at his restless walking about, pacing the length of the lobby back and forth, like a caged animal.

'Jane!' The one word was ejected like the shot from a gun. 'Oh, the relief! I was terrified that you wouldn't come.' He looked at her, taking in the smart little suit of apple-green linen, the wide-brimmed sun-hat in straw, made by one of the vendors in the native market just along the street, the white sandals and matching shoulder bag. Something touched his memory and he winced. But as she watched his changing expression Jane knew for sure that the vision before him had been transposed by the one of the girl he had loved.

'I oughtn't to have come,' she frowned, moving from the lobby to enter the lounge. 'What is it you want me for, Don?' He had followed, standing until she sat down at a low table in a secluded corner out of sight of people entering the hotel. He sat down after beckoning to a passing waiter and ordering drinks—whisky for himself and a dry sherry for Jane.

'I want to talk about us,' he said presently. 'You've no future here, in Mauritius. You say that the children won't be needing you much longer; you say too that this man you're engaged to will never entertain the idea of marriage with a divorcee.' He glanced at her across the table, saw her small hands clasped tightly, the ring adorning one beautifully-manicured finger. 'Neither of us has much to live for at present,' he continued, 'so we might as well get together again and try to build something worthwhile. Time will help us, Jane, time and forgiveness.'

Time, yes. Forgiveness was on her side alone; Don had nothing to forgive. She realised she was being bitter and switched her thoughts to Philippe, who was deliberately avoiding her, who had not asked for an explanation but accepted what he saw as inexcusable, the conduct of a wanton, almost, a girl who had come very close to surrender on more than one occasion. It all looked black against her, and she felt weighed down, drained of all desire to vindicate herself. For what would it profit her to try to explain? She had practised deceit, had lied several times, and even last night, out there on the shore, she had, in her desperation, lied even yet again, introducing Don as a friend, distantly related. It was too much to expect forgiveness, or even understanding. In any case, Philippe would consider both those to be superfluous, seeing that she would never mean anything to him.

Don was paying the waiter; she found herself staring down into amber liquid which caught the light as she absently moved the glass in circles, vaguely hearing

the chatter of voices in several tongues, coming from
various parts of the lounge.

'Jane. . . . ' Don's voice intruded into her trance-like
mood and she lifted her lashes, meeting his gaze, recalling with poignant intensity the days when she had
first met him and a look like that could thrill her
through and through.

She had believed it to be love, and so had Don.

She waited in silence for him to continue and eventually he was asking her again if she would return to
him, let him take her back with him in two weeks'
time.

'It won't work,' she said, but her statement lacked
strength.

'With time it will.'

'How long, Don? How much of our lives must we
waste before peace comes to us?'

'Peace?' The glass was halfway to his mouth but he
put it down on the table again. 'That's a strange word
to use, Jane.'

'Peace of mind. How long will it take you to forget
Gina?'

No answer. She saw the twist of pain on his face
the shadows that darkened the blue of his eyes. She
said after a moment of silence,

'Do you suppose I shall fare any better? Are you
expecting me to forget Philippe in a few weeks, or
even months?'

'There was nothing between you, and you admitted
he's never told you he loves you, even though he
believed you were single and free to marry him. Surely
that proves there's nothing really deep between you

It was different with Gina and me; we were together—
really together——'

'All right, Don,' she cut in tersely. 'You've said it
all before.'

'Sorry, Jane. I don't think I'm hurting you.'

'You're not,' she retorted. 'I've an armour now. One
does acquire one, you know. It's like the animals.
Nature gives you self-protection as it does them.'

'You're bitter,' he observed, taking a drink and putting down the glass. 'I can't blame you, though.'

'I'd be a cynic, too, if it wasn't for my love for
Philippe.'

He frowned, compressing his lips.

'You'll get over it. You've not known him five
minutes.'

Keeping her eyes fixed on his face, Jane said,

'You're weakening your case, Don. I won't have
you adopting that tone when you talk about Philippe.'

A sneer caught his underlip.

'He's wealthy—a millionaire?'

Jane's eyes glinted.

'Shall we change the subject, Don?'

'I'm sorry.' He heaved a sigh, took another drink
and said contritely, 'It's none of my business—his
money, I mean.'

'Nor anything else about him.'

'Except that he's been kissing my wife!'

'Oh, for heaven's sake!' she cried. 'People in glass
houses don't throw stones—or they shouldn't!'

He bit his lip, closing his eyes as if he wanted to
enter into complete darkness.

'I must be going.' Jane looked at her wristwatch,

then drained her glass. 'Bhoosan's waiting for me in the car park.'

'I've hired a car. I'd like to run you to the chateau.'

She shook her head.

'I'll go with Bhoosan——' She stopped abruptly, her gaze fixed on the girl who had just entered the lounge. Yvette!

She spotted Jane on the instant and came over, her curious glance moving swiftly to Don, who was finishing his drink.

'Miss Clark.' That was all, then silence. She was waiting for an invitation to join them. Had she forgotten what happened the last time they met? She had insulted Jane and Philippe had apologised on her behalf. Well, whether she had forgotten or not, she wasn't allowing the incident to trouble her.

'A friend?' queried Don hesitantly.

'A friend of Monsieur de Chameral. Miss Sutcliffe, meet my friend, Donald Clark.'

'Clark? You're related?'

'I believe we're cousins about a dozen times removed,' replied Don, who seemed to resent the girl's intrusion.

'Not related at all, then?'

Jane, realising that she was ten minutes late already, rose from her chair, nodded coldly to Yvette, and said goodbye to Don.

'But——' He hurried after her, catching her up in the lobby. It occurred to Jane that the girl would be curious about such behaviour and she turned with a frown to say shortly,

'I don't like that girl! She'll be suspecting something....' Her voice trailed. What did it matter if

Yvette suspected something? 'I must go, Don.' Jane's voice had softened a little, and her gaze was compassionate. 'What are you going to do for the rest of the day?'

He shook his head dumbly, and closed his eyes.

'I wish I were dead....'

'Don't, Don—oh, please don't say such things! There'll be a lot to live for one day. You said yourself that time will heal the wound.'

He looked at her through glazed eyes.

'If you would help me, Jane?' It was another cry from the heart, a terrible, agonising plea on which his whole life seemed to depend.

And as she stared into his eyes Jane suddenly became afraid ... afraid that he would find release by his own hand. An urgency entered into her and she heard herself saying impulsively,

'Look, Don, I'm free after the children are in bed—that's about eight o'clock. I'll meet you outside the gates of the chateau——'

'Jane!' he burst in, 'thank you! Thank you for your pity and your kindness.' And in his gratitude he kissed her cheek, there in the busy lobby of the hotel.

As she glanced over his shoulder Jane's eyes met those of Yvette, who had come from the lounge and was standing, motionless, to one side of the wide doorway that separated the lounge from the lobby.

There was no sign of Philippe when Jane returned to the chateau, driven there by Bhoosan, who had chatted to her as they travelled through the vast region of sugar canes. The sun was brilliant, but the south-east trade winds, which blew from April to October, provided a cooling breeze which drifted in through the open windows of the car. Bhoosan had related the tear-jerking story of Paul and Virginia, the tragedy of two lovers parted, never to come together again. Their story was the creation of Bernardin de Saint Pierre and their statues formed a beautiful picture, set as it was amid a pretty water scene in the town of Port Louis. It was not the kind of story Jane wanted to hear at a time like this, but she was reluctant to interrupt the story which the chauffeur was so obviously enjoying telling her.

But the result was that she felt even more unhappy than ever as she entered the chateau, and the discovery that Philippe was still evading her only added to her dejection. Life had lost its zest; there seemed only one course open to her and that was to go back to Don and make a concerted effort to repair at least some of the damage that had been done in the past few months. Her pity was very much with her husband; she felt sure he needed her desperately and that if she deserted him there was no knowing what he might do.

Her decision was made that evening when Meri came to her and said that she had had instructions that Mademoiselle was tired and wanted her dinner in her sitting-room.

Her first reaction was to inform the maid that she was going out, but she realised instantly that this would arouse her curiosity, such action being at variance with Philippe's assertion that she was tired.

'Thank you, Meri. I'll have it brought up a little early, immediately after the children are in bed.'

'Certainly, mademoiselle.'

'And—Meri. . . .'

The girl turned at the door.

'Yes, mademoiselle?'

'Don't let anyone come to my room afterwards. The tray can be taken away in the morning.'

'Very good, mademoiselle.'

It was Rima who brought up the tray, commenting anxiously on Jane's supposed tiredness.

'It's those two, miss,' she stated. 'They're so boisterous at times. I think, miss, you should let Meri or me have them sometimes.'

Jane smiled and thanked her for her concern.

'They're a handful, I admit, but never too much for me, Rima. After all, they're at school for several hours a day, so I do have a break. And I have my evenings, of course.'

The girl had placed the tray with its heated dishes on a table by the sofa, then she stood looking at Jane, who realised she wanted to say something.

'What is it, Rima?'

'Monseigneur has told us that the children's father will be coming to take them away soon?'

'That's right. He wants them to live with him. Their place is with their father, of course.'

The girl swallowed. Both she and Meri had grown to love Barry and Tamsin and it was not difficult to see that Rima at least was going to be upset at the parting.

'When is he coming, miss?'

'I believe it will be in a few weeks' time.'

'A few weeks? Monseigneur said that it would be a few days.'

Jane blinked at her.

'He did?'

'Yes, miss. It's a wonder he hasn't told you—when he told us.'

'Does Bhoosan know?'

'Perhaps not, miss.'

The girl went then, closing the door silently behind her. Jane stared at it thoughtfully. Mr Scott had written, then, and he was coming to Mauritius soon. Well, it all seemed to be fitting in ... all was designed to shape her fate, her actions and decisions.

She took some of the food from the dishes, put it on a plate, then tucked it into a plastic bag she had. The dessert was treated in the same way, then the bag was enclosed in another and finally put into a piece of brown paper. She did not trouble much about her appearance, merely brushing her hair and putting on a clean blouse and cotton skirt. With her handbag over her shoulder and the parcel in her hand, she made her way along the verandah to the steps at the end. Within a couple of minutes she was walking briskly through the starlit grounds of the chateau towards the gate. Don was there; she saw the dark outline of the car, with Don standing beside it, the glow of his cigarette bright red in the darkness. He never used to smoke, she recalled, and wondered what kind of comfort he was deriving from smoking now. Gina had probably smoked and that was what had started Don off.

'Jane, it's a relief to see you!' There was no mistaking that relief as he tossed away the half-smoked cigarette. 'We're going somewhere for dinner, aren't we? You can't have eaten already?'

She shook her head, getting into the car when he opened the door for her. Their hands touched and she frowned. And an hour later she was saying, after they had talked about their future over the first course of their dinner,

'I'm not prepared to take up exactly where we left off, Don. You can't expect it.'

He looked at her swiftly.

'It's to be—platonic?'

She nodded.

'Yes, I'm afraid so. I love Philippe.' Simplicity in the words, but for her they savoured of eloquence because of the underlying emotion that filled her as she uttered them. It was not an emotion of the heart, but of the mind and body. Her heart was dead.

'I'll have to agree.' He was frowning, and she saw with a little access of apprehension that a strange light shone in his eyes, fierce, glittering, then it was gone, extinguished by a terrible shadow of hopelessness. 'Perhaps you were right when you said it won't work.' He had been going to butter a roll, but he stopped, the knife idle in his hand, tossed the roll back into the basket from which he had taken it. 'I'm not hungry! Let's get out of here!' He was distraught, Jane realised, convinced that if they went from the restaurant into the gardens surrounding it there would be another outburst, similar to the one that had occurred last night when in his terrible grief he had flung himself on to the ground and wept as if his heart would break. The memory brought tears to her eyes, a quiver to her lips.

'I'm hungry, Don,' she said, injecting a note of apology into her voice. 'Do you mind if I finish my dinner?'

He became calm instantly. There was no doubt, she mused, that she had a certain influence over him. He knew it, too, and that was why he needed her, desperately.

'No, of course I don't mind. I'm sorry, Jane, very sorry. Forgive me and try to be patient and understanding. I have no one now but you——' His eyes were moist as they met hers across the table. 'Come to—to th-think of it, I'm hungry too.'

She contrived a smile, though she did not know how.

'In that case, let's both enjoy it. You must admit that this Guyanese food is really delicious.'

CHAPTER NINE

WHEN the meal was finished they went into the lounge, where Jane had a glass of lemonade and Don drank far too much whisky.

'You're driving,' she reminded him. 'Don't have any more.'

He lit a cigarette and inhaled deeply.

'I can take it,' he assured her tersely. 'I've got used to it over these past few months.'

'During the time you were parted from Gina?'

'And when we were together. She enjoyed a drink.'

Enjoyed too many drinks, Jane almost said, but checked herself abruptly, and fell silent, watching him take the smoke deeply into his lungs and then exhale slowly, dangerously.

'It's time we were going,' she said at last. 'I don't want to be too late.'

He made no comment, but beckoned the waiter who was attending the next table.

'You say you've not seen this man, Philippe, yet—not since he stalked off last evening?'

'No, I haven't. I told you in the car.'

'You want to see him as soon as possible. Tell him you're leaving with me. We could leave in a few days. There's no need to wait till the fortnight's up.'

'I'm not leaving the children yet. I promised to come back to you, but I didn't say when. I'm staying till Mr Scott arrives to take Barry and Tasmin—if Philippe wants me to stay, that is,' she thought to add. She would not be surprised if he told her to leave immediately, as there was always Meri and Rima who could take care of the children for a short while. She had mentioned the two girls to Don and it was no surprise to her to hear him say,

'There are the two maids who can have the kids.'

'I'm their nanny. I'll leave when Philippe tells me to.'

He was about to say something when the waiter came up. Don ordered whisky, then looked at Jane, who shook her head, a deep sigh escaping her. The future looked bleak enough without her having to put up with her husband's heavy drinking—for it was obvious that he had become a heavy drinker, and a heavy smoker.

'I wonder what the aristocratic Frenchman will think when he learns that you're married.' Don spoke derisively and it was all Jane could do to hold her temper.

'I'm dreading the meeting,' was all she said for the moment, but presently she was adding, 'I'll be relieved to get the confession off my mind, though.'

Don looked at her speculatively.

'He was kissing you,' he mused, 'and you were liking it.'

She swallowed, her face pale but oddly composed.

'I've told you, I love him.'

'More than you loved me?'

Impatience looked out of her eyes but was hidden from her voice.

'If you must know,' she answered frankly, 'yes, more than I loved you. Ours was a shallow thing, Don, and it will never change, no matter how long we live together. What I feel for Philippe is deep ... deep within my heart ... here....' She was lost in a dream, with Philippe close and Don a million miles away. 'I'd give my life for him—willingly.' Her eyes lifted and met those of her husband. 'Love, real love, is like that. But there could never be anything permanent between Philippe and me because, as I said, he'd never marry a divorcee, much as he loves me——' She broke off abruptly, a hand stealing to her lips, her glance taking in the odd expression that had come to her husband's face.

'He loves you? You gave me to understand that he didn't.'

She shook her head.

'It was never mentioned.'

'No,' he agreed reflectively, 'but I somehow got the impression that the affair was one-sided, that you had a crush on your handsome employer——'

'It's not a crush,' she interrupted angrily. 'I'd rather not talk about him, if you don't mind!'

Don downed the whole of the whisky as if it were nothing stronger than the lemonade his wife had been drinking. He lifted a finger to a waiter and ordered another whisky, a double. Jane said in despair,

'You'll never be able to drive the car, Don. For goodness' sake stop. It's no good to you in quantities like that.'

'I said I can take it. Tell me some more about this Philippe. How do you know he's in love with you?'

'I suppose,' she answered thoughtfully after a long pause, 'that I'm not really sure; I only thought I was, owing to the way he looked at me, and spoke, tenderly, gently, without the sort of cold superiority he'd adopted towards me at first. And his lovemaking——'

'Lovemaking? You swore there'd been nothing!'

She looked at him coolly.

'There was nothing—intimate. I meant, the way he held me and kissed me.' She stopped, reflecting that, had her husband not put in that untimely appearance, Philippe might have declared his love. At the time she felt sure he loved her ... but now.... Doubts had crept in unwanted; they were gnawing all the time. As before she sighed for what might have been but was admitting that, the circumstances being what they were, there was not the remotest chance of any future for her and Philippe. She was resigned anyway to going back to England and to the home which was still there, the home which she and Don had made together, in the days when they were happy, and optimistic regarding the future.

It was all so sad that the break came in the first place, as if it hadn't they would have gone on, living a happy life together, blissfully ignorant of what they were missing. The appearance of Gina on the scene, beautiful and sexy, had brought home to Don the deficiencies in his marriage, and he had immediately set about doing something about it. The advent of Philippe in Jane's life had had a similar effect, but in her case there was nothing she could do about it. Philippe was not for her any more than Gina was meant for Don.

'It's obvious that it isn't a crush you have.' Don's voice, quiet and thoughtful, broke her reverie and she glanced across at him, noticing for the first time that the collar of his shirt was not quite clean. He had always been so particular....

'I said I don't want to talk about him, Don.'

'You have been talking about him, though, just now.'

There was a strange silence, with Don still thoughtful, and hesitant. But at length he spoke, slowly, watching his wife's expression all the time.

'After you'd left the Stag Hotel today that woman, Miss Sutcliffe, had a drink with me——'

'She did? I thought you were leaving directly after I did?'

'I intended to, but she came to me and was all charm. She suggested we have a drink together. I discovered that she was the woman whom you'd talked about, the one the Frenchman was supposed to marry, on account of his making that promise to his friend.'

'She told you that?'

He nodded.

'She told me lots of things. I soon caught on to the reason why you didn't like her. She's a bitch—hates you like poison and would do you an injury if she could. She was fishing and that's why she put on the charm. She was dying to know about us, said you'd had letters from England, from a man—— How did she know it was a man?'

'Handwriting; you can always tell.'

'She tries to be clever but isn't. I soon gathered that she was jealous of you right from the start, and that she'd very much have liked to read one of those letters. She'd stayed at the chateau, hadn't she?'

'Yes, for a fortnight.' A thoughtful silence followed before Jane said, 'I always kept your letters locked in my suitcase.'

'You think she'd have gone into your room?'

'It would be a despicable trick,' frowned Jane.

'She's capable of anything, that one. I wouldn't trust her as far as I could throw her!' He looked at his empty glass. 'Keep me company, Jane; have something—another lemonade, perhaps?'

'I hate your drinking like this, Don,' she said without answering his question. 'Are you going to give it up when we get back home?'

'Can't. Impossible.' A waiter happened to be passing and he ordered another double whisky for himself and a lemonade for Jane. 'It does something for you,' he resumed, staring at the waiter's retreating back. 'Makes you forget. You ought to try it—maybe you will, so as to forget this dashing Frenchman....' He was slurring his words! it amazed Jane that he wasn't roaring drunk already. She thought of the hired car standing there, in the hotel park, and decided she would have to drive him back to his hotel herself and then take the car back to the chateau, from where he would have to collect it in the morning—or she might take it to him, having Bhoosan drive behind and pick her up. A deep sigh escaped her. Why did Don have to drown his sorrows in drink? She could sympathise, of course, but she felt that as long as she was willing to make such a great sacrifice for him he should do something for her. She had no wish to have him go out after dinner and come staggering home at bedtime, which was what she imagined would happen if he did not cut down a bit.

'That woman, Miss Sutcliffe——— She told me to call her Yvette.' Don's eyes were on the waiter who had come back, to thread his way to their table. 'She was probing all the time. I didn't tell her anything, just said we were friends and as I'd come to Mauritius for a holiday I thought I'd look you up.'

'It sounds a bit weak, after you'd been writing to me regularly.' Although three letters had arrived from Don while Yvette was at the chateau and as luck would have it she had picked up them all.

'It would keep her guessing.' He put a hand in his pocket to pay the waiter. Jane's eyes widened at the tip. Don was past knowing what he was doing, obviously, as the tip was far more than the cost of the drinks. 'She might get back with your Frenchman once you're out of her way.' He lifted the glass. 'Cheers! To a happy married life together——' The glass slid from his hand to crash on to the table. Jane, ashamed as she had never been before, apologised to the waiter, saying that her companion was ill. Don was leaning back against the upholstery of his chair, both hands to his face ... and when presently he drew them down, past his chin to his throat, she saw that there were tears in his eyes.

He babbled all the way to his hotel, mainly about Yvette, repeatedly asserting that she would do Jane an injury if she could.

'Watch her,' he slurred when at last Jane had got him to the hotel and out of the car. 'I'm not intoxicated, you know. I can take it.'

'You weren't fit to drive the car.'

'That's what you said, but if you hadn't been there I'd have had to drive it, wouldn't I?'

'You could have got a taxi—— Don, you mustn't get like this again——'

'I've been like it many a time!'

'You mustn't drive—promise me.'

He was silent, staring up at the lights of his hotel.

'My room's up there——' He pointed. 'Come on up—it's early, and after all you are my wife.'

Sickened, she entered the lobby to get help. It was there instantly in the shape of a strong young Creole porter.

'My friend's not too well,' she told him, vaguely wondering what he would think of her excuse once he saw her husband. 'Please get him safely to his room.' She gave him a generous tip for which he thanked her, flashing several gold teeth.

'Leave it to me,' he responded cheerfully. 'We do sometimes have to help guests who are ill.'

So he had guessed already, without even seeing the man he was to assist.

Jane said goodnight and drove off without even looking back. Her heart was beating overrate at the experience of seeing the husband she had once loved reduced to the degrading state he was in tonight. Life would be hell, she thought bitterly, and for a moment she resolved to break her promise to him. But her mood changed as pity overwhelmed her. Tomorrow he would feel awful, both physically and mentally. He did need help; she was his wife, who had married him for better or worse. . . . .

Already drained and sunk into the deepest abyss of misery, Jane had no wish to meet Philippe tonight. But he was there when she drove the car on to the forecourt, standing like a statue on the marble steps, framed between gleaming white pillars, the light behind him throwing his severely-cut features into shadow, giving them an almost satanic look. She had thought of driving the car to the back, but decided against it, convinced that, should Philippe see it, he would immediately come to the conclusion that she had been attempting to hide it away, out of sight, and with the intention of removing it in the morning before he saw it. She was glad now that she had brought it to the front, because, standing there as he was, he would have been sure to hear the engine as she drove along the avenue from the gate to the chateau.

He was still motionless when, having alighted from the driver's seat, she advanced slowly up the steps. She expected him to move and when he remained there she was forced to stop. This she did, but coming too close for comfort, having mounted one step too many. He towered above her, majestic and arrogant, the master of the Chateau de Chameral and the vast estate attached to it.

He was the first to break the silence, as Jane had meant him to—mainly because she herself was tongue-tied, unable to collect her thoughts, much less find something suitable to say to him.

'You've got back, then.' With a sort of slow deliberation he glanced at his watch. 'Do you know the time, Jane?'

She gripped the strap of her shoulder bag, fumbling for words. All she could find to say was that she was sorry it was so late and then, as she saw his eyes look down, beyond her shoulder to the car, she added flatly, 'That's a hired car. Don wasn't well enough to drive it back to his hotel, so I took him.' Why didn't he move, she wondered irritably, and let her pass him?'

'You've been with your friend?'

'Yes, I——'

'Meri thought you were tired!' he snapped. 'She'll know you've been out!'

'*I* didn't tell her I was tired.' She had no inclination to tell him of her ruse and that Meri would never know she had not eaten her dinner and then gone to bed. 'Can—can I pass you—Philippe?'

No answer; his eyes were fixed upon her finger, the third finger of her left hand.

'Where's your ring?' he demanded in a very soft voice. 'Why aren't you wearing it?'

She was so weary, with a cloud of tears behind her eyes and the weight of utter despair in her heart, that she found it impossible to stand here answering his questions. And on sudden impulse she took another step, brushed unceremoniously past him and entered the brilliantly-lit hall of the chateau. Vaguely things registered—familiar things like the marble floor and high wide window framed in gold brocade, the delicately-carved furniture harmonising so perfectly despite the fact that various pieces were from different eras and countries. She saw the silver bowls of flowers on gleaming antique tables, the silver candelabra, the golden-crowned model of the Virgin and Child, this latter a vivid reminder that the noble owner of this chateau would never marry a divorcee. He was old-fashioned in his ideas and she loved him all the more for it. But tonight she knew an impatience born of utter dejection and she had no time even for the man who, in the bleak and sunless future, would be forever in her thoughts.

She turned misty eyes towards him, straining to combat the great difference in their heights. He had

closed the door and was once more standing motionless, like a judge, dark condemnation in his eyes. Anger
flared, out of control. Jane prudently said a stiff goodnight and would have mounted the stairs if Philippe
had not stopped her, moving with the speed of a jungle
cat and grasping her wrist, jerking it cruelly in order
to bring her round to face him.

'I asked you where your ring was?' he gritted. 'Why
aren't you wearing it—answer me at once!'

She stared, conscious of a throbbing in her brain.
Oh, God, if only she could lie on her pillow, and
become unconscious of everything—the troubles of the
present and the frightening uncertainties of the future.

But it was not to be. One swift glance at her cap-
tor's savage expression was sufficient to convince her
of the futility of ignoring his questions.

'We're not really engaged, Philippe, so I feel I can
stop wearing it. I'll—I'll give it back to you tomorrow.'
She stopped, recoiling from the fury in his gaze.

'You took it off because you were going out with that
friend of yours! Who is he? What is he to you?' The
pressure on her wrist increased painfully and she
winced, trying unsuccessfully to free herself from his
grasp.

'I want to talk to you about Don,' she said wearily,
'but not tonight—please, Philippe, not tonight.'

His face was a mask of fury, but the expression in
his eyes had changed, and as she looked into them she
knew without any doubt at all that the poison darts of
jealousy were torturing him. She had not been mistaken in believing that he loved her. No, indeed, for his
suffering at this moment was equally as grievous as
hers.

'You—are in love with him?' A pallor had risen under the bronze of his skin and in his throat a nerve jerked spasmodically, out of control. 'You were in his arms——' Philippe stopped, black fury in his eyes. 'Did you not tell him you were engaged to me?'

'Philippe ... our engagement wasn't real—I mean, you know why we—— Why you wanted it.' That this was a stupid thing to say failed to register until afterwards, when she realised that there was not the slightest need to remind him of why he wanted it.

'At first out engagement wasn't real, but you must have known that I——' Abruptly he stopped, his nostrils flaring at the knowledge of what he had been on the point of admitting. His whole manner changed, dramatically, unbelievably, for he was calm all at once, having resumed that old familiar air of arrogant superiority and cold indifference. 'Mr Scott has written to me; his plans have changed. He'll be here the day after tomorrow.' His chill incisive tone was a dagger in Jane's heart and impulsively she flung out her hands to him in a gesture of desperate pleading.

'I'll talk to you—now—about Don—if you want me to! I intended talking earlier but couldn't find you. And you t-told Meri that—that I was tired and wanted my dinner upstairs, so I hadn't the courage to—to come and talk. Why did you avoid me, Philippe? You must have known that there was some sort of an explanation——'

'You were with this fellow Clark during the afternoon,' he cut in harshly. 'This morning I was called away, urgently, to the office on the plantation and went early, before breakfast, and was there until after lunch. Yvette called here later, to tell me you were at the

Stag Hotel with your friend. She questioned him, apparently, when you had left, and although he did not tell her much, she deduced that he's the man who's been writing to you regularly. I did ask you, at the time I wanted you to become engaged to me, if you were engaged to anyone else, and you said no.'

'It was true. Don was not—not my fiancé.'

'Your lover, then?' he queried in a very soft tone of voice. And when she made no answer, 'I could have been your lover, couldn't I?' Contempt brought an ugly twist to his mouth. 'You're shameless, Jane, and I don't want you in my house. You are free to go— and I would prefer it to be soon.' A pause to give her a chance to speak, but she shook her head, torn to pieces by the torture inflicted on her by two men— this one and her husband. Physical and emotional fatigue robbed her of everything except the desperate craving for solitude, for the sanctuary of her room where she could shed the tears that were causing this unbearable throbbing in her temples. She looked at him through eyes that could scarcely see; his face was blurred and all that registered was the sombre frown creasing his brow ... and that nerve pulsating in his throat.

'I must go to bed,' she quivered, turning to place a trembling hand on the balustrade rail. 'Goodnight— Monseigneur.'

There was no answer and she hadn't expected one. As she reached the first curve of the magnificent staircase she paused momentarily to look down. Philippe had gone, and all she saw was the drawing-room door gently closing on its hinges.

Once in her room all control left her and she flung

herself on the bed and wept bitterly. For it all to end like this, without Philippe ever knowing the truth, never discovering that she was not nearly so blame-worthy as he believed. Yet as she had told herself before, it did not really matter. When she left here they would never meet again, their paths would be severed for ever.

It was a long while later that she rose from the bed and went to the window, flinging it wide open. She wanted air, cool and soothing as it blew in from the crystal clear waters of the lagoon. It shone in the star-light, like a sheet of pure silver, with just a small shadow where, on the shore, a beautiful feathery casua-rina tree spread its foliage over the shoreline where it narrowed at the far end of the crescent. Her eyes moved, to the grounds of the chateau, bathed in moonlight that was fading but still shedding a muted argent glow over the silent landscape. She would miss it all so much! She had little known, when she had accepted the re-sponsibility of bringing Barry and Tamsin over here, just what havoc the action was to play in her life. But that was fate. Philippe had spoken once of fate. And he had spoken of truth as well. Truth ... it takes two to find it, he had stated, one to speak it and one to understand it.

And he had not given her the chance to speak the truth to him. If he had, then perhaps he would have understood, and forgiven her.

She was up very early the following morning, having lain awake for most of the night. She had come to the conclusion that it would be best to leave that day, so she was packing by eight o'clock, having already had her bath and a cup of tea brought up by Meri.

She felt her mind was in a state of total inertia; she was unable to think at all, and the result was that the idea of saying goodbye to the children had no emotional effect upon her at all. Everything was automatic, as if she were a robot controlled by some outside force that guided her actions without her being conscious of performing them.

The children had been told that their daddy was coming to take them to live with them, and to Jane's surprise Barry, at least, seemed happy at the news. He chatted at the breakfast table about all the things his daddy used to do for them.

'He played with us in the garden and took us to the fair—— Do you remember, Tamsin?' His sister was eating slowly and made no answer. 'She's sulking again because she doesn't want to go away from here.'

'I'm not sulking! I don't want a new mummy—I want Auntie Jane instead!'

'A new mummy?' Jane glanced from Tamsin to her brother. 'Are you having a new mummy?'

'Uncle Philippe said yesterday that when our daddy comes he's bringing a lady what's going to be married to him.'

A new mummy.... In a flash Jane's mind cleared and she was able to think. And all her fears for the children's happiness returned. So many things to trouble her! Would she ever know peace again?

'What else did Uncle Philippe say?'

'That our daddy's going to have a nice new house in the country and we're going to live there.' Suddenly his eyes shadowed and his lip trembled. 'I don't want to leave you, Auntie Jane, but I want to see my daddy because I love him. Why can't you come and live with us and be our new mummy?'

'It isn't possible, darling. I have my own home to go to.'

'Will you come and see us, then?'

'Are you going to live in England?'

'Yes, but not where we used to live. Daddy has told Uncle Philippe that it's going to be in the country, and we'll have fields to play in.'

'Then I shall come and see you, Barry, many times.' That at least would be something in her life, a ray of brightness in the gloom.

She got them ready for school and saw them off, a terrible ache in her heart at the knowledge that this was goodbye for the present. She supposed she would learn, some time, where they were living.

'See you later!' cried Barry as he waved from the car.

The same words every morning. . . . She had become so used to them. The break was inevitable, though, since their father's intention was to have them with him.

She returned to her room, packed another suitcase and then put them all in the car Don had hired. To leave like this! Would she see Philippe or would she have to leave a note?

And what about the servants? Meri would be hurt and so would Rima, if she went off without a word. And there was Bhoosan and Silva. What explanation was Philippe intending to give, Jane wondered, but the next moment she was telling herself that it was not her business; she had enough problems of her own without overtaxing her mind with other people's.

She was ready, standing by the door of her bedroom looking round. She had been happy here at first, before all the problems had reared their ugly heads. Well, she would soon be away and the forgetting time could begin ... but how long? The way she felt at this moment of leaving the chateau she thought the memory of Philippe would be with her till the end of her days.

And the sheer horror of it all was that she would be living with another man, her husband whom she no longer loved but whose prop she would always be.

Turning from the room she closed the door, then went to the kitchen to find the two maids. Meri was there, but Rima was having a day off to visit her mother in Curepipe.

'I'm leaving, Meri, and want to say goodbye—and thank you for all the things you've done for me and the children.'

The girl just gaped at her unbelievingly.

'Leaving, mademoiselle? But I don't know what you mean. The children are going, yes, but you—you are now engaged to Monseigneur. I do not understand you, mademoiselle.'

'Monseigneur will explain,' returned Jane gently, biting her lip as Meri's eyes filled with tears. 'I must leave,' she said. 'It's quite impossible that I can stay any longer.' And without giving the maid an opportunity of asking any questions she went from the kitchen into the hall, where she came face to face with Philippe. His eyes were cold, like steel, but there was something else there as well, something that made her want to fling her arms around his neck and weep on his shoulder. For she read bitter disillusionment in

his eyes and his face was tinged with grey, as if he had
been ill for some considerable time.

'Philippe ... may I write to you ... please?'

The idea had only just come, but it was one she
wanted to carry out. A letter would at least explain
some of the reasons for what she had done; it would
also explain her relationship with Don and Philippe
would learn that her husband depended on her—in
fact, his life depended on her; this Jane knew without
the slightest doubt at all.

'I'd rather you didn't.'

She held out her hand and to her surprise he took
it.

'I've left your ring on the dressing-table, Philippe,'
she said. 'Goodbye, and be—be h-happy!' She would
have run from him, but he caught her hand again and
kept it firmly in his.

'Jane, where are you going? I saw that your suitcases were in the car you brought home last night.
Where are you going?' he asked again, his voice quiet
and hoarse, without any hint of anger or condemnation.

'To—to Don's hotel,' she replied. 'There isn't anywhere else—— You see, I've got to get a flight. ...' Her
voice failed altogether; she made no effort to continue,
for words were so inadequate in a situation like this. He
had released her hand, at the same time putting distance between them. Jane felt that if she could only
go to him, put both her hands in his and her head
against his breast, there would be no need for words;
he would instantly realise that there was so much he
did not know.

But such action on her part was not permissible. He

would recoil from her ... or would he ...?

She looked at him, aware of a tensely hesitant quality in his whole manner which caused her to wait, breathlessly, in an agony of suspense ... for something to happen, but she had no idea what.

'Jane——'. His mouth twisted on the word. 'Jane——' He broke off again and sighed. And when he spoke a second later his voice was cold, his face a mask. 'What have you said to the children?'

'They'll be expecting me to be here when they come home from school,' she answered, and he frowned.

'They don't know you're leaving?'

She shook her head; it was aching abominably and she automatically brushed her hair from her forehead. The action caught his whole attention and he seemed fascinated by the gleaming cascade of hair round her face.

'It's best this way, Philippe. Barry's quite resigned to going to live with his daddy. As you said, there seems to have been a very happy rapport between him and his father. Tamsin might take longer to adjust, but I'm sure she will eventually. I've promised to visit them, if I can get their address. I imagine Mr Scott will be in touch with Mrs Davis, so I shall probably get his address from her.'

Philippe merely nodded. Jane murmured another goodbye and wondered if he would see her to the door.

But at that moment the bell rang and when he opened it Yvette was there, a sort of triumphant satisfaction on her face.

'I just thought I'd call in as I was passing.' There was barely a glance for Philippe, as her eyes were on Jane, who had a small overnight bag in her hand and a coat over her arm. 'You're going somewhere, Miss Clark?' There was no mistaking the emphasis on the 'Miss', nor the perceptive quality of the girl's voice. She knew.... But how?

Philippe said slowly and with apparent difficulty,

'Miss Clark's leaving, Yvette. You might as well know that our engagement's at an end.' His eyes, expressionless and cold, stared unseeingly at the wall behind Yvette.

His humiliation must be terrible to bear, thought Jane, herself excruciatingly hurt. She hated this girl for turning up at this particular time. Why had she come anyway? Jane caught her unguarded expression and with a sudden flash of insight she was positive that Yvette had a motive ... an invidious one.

And within seconds she was to learn what it was.

'Well, the engagement was a sham, wasn't it, Philippe?' He gave a start, but before he could speak Yvette was saying, 'For one thing, this woman's married——'

'Married?' He shook his head, as if his brain were in a ferment of disbelief fighting with acceptance. It soon became clear, though, that enlightenment about several things was coming to him. 'Is this true, Jane?'

'She hasn't told you?' broke in Yvette sneeringly. 'I thought she would have told you by now—before she left——' She stopped momentarily and when she resumed her tone had become softly malevolent as she said, 'You see, Philippe, she's going back to her husband.'

A terrible silence followed before Philippe, having miraculously regained full command of himself, becoming at once the noble, distinguished Frenchman whom Jane had first encountered, said in tones of icy politeness,

'I won't keep you, Jane. You have everything?'

She nodded dumbly, lowering her head to hide the tears in her eyes. 'Then I'll bid you goodbye.'

'G-good—good-b-bye....' Without a glance for the woman who had come here deliberately to hurt and humiliate them both, Jane made her way blindly to the door, passed through it, and heard it close quietly behind her.

CHAPTER TEN

SHE arrived to find Don still in bed, but he was with her in the lounge half an hour after she had phoned his room from the lobby. She wasted no time in relating what had transpired, from the time she arrived back at the chateau last night, when Philippe was waiting for her, to the incident an hour or so ago when Yvette had arrived on the scene just as Jane was leaving, and told Philippe that Jane was married and going back to her husband. He listened in complete silence, and as she watched his face Jane noticed the heavy frown that spread over his forehead and the guilty colour creeping into his cheeks.

'How did she learn all that?' questioned Jane finally, her alert gaze still fixed on his face. He seemed little the worse for the heavy drinking of last night, although there was a haggard look about him as if he hadn't slept very well.

'I'm afraid it was all my fault, Jane.' The confession came after a kind of agitated silence. 'I shot my mouth off last night——'

'Last night? But you were going to bed when I left you——' Jane stopped, impatient with herself for the interruption. 'You didn't go to bed. What happened?'

'I wanted another drink, so I came in here. Miss Sutcliffe was here with her parents—she introduced them to me. They'd been dining out to celebrate her mother's birthday or something. I can't remember, with my mind being so fuddled. Well, her parents disappeared for a few minutes—— Oh, yes, some friends must have come in for a late drink and called them over to their table. It left that bitchy piece with me; she started asking questions—saw I was a bit plastered and knew I'd talk, fool that I was!'

'You told her—everything?'

'I expect so; she seemed to know it all. I can't remember what the devil I said.' He was angry with himself and yet a moment later he gave a crooked smile and asked if it really mattered all that much. 'You won't be seeing this French bloke again, so why worry? Personally, I think he's got more in common with that Yvette woman than he has with you. They're both damned snobbish, for one thing.'

Jane swallowed hard, almost hating her husband for the way he talked. He did not seem to realise the emptiness she was experiencing, the unbearable agony of knowing she would never again see the man she loved. How could he couple Philippe's name with that of Yvette? Had he no idea at all of sparing her feelings? Once again the future terrified her—the bleak path she was destined to tread, a man beside her whom she did not love, and who had no love for her.

'The children's father should be coming for them some time tomorrow,' she said flatly, wanting to change the subject. 'I've promised to visit them. Mr Scott's going to buy a house somewhere in England.'

'You'd do well to forget everything to do with this island, Jane,' frowned Don. 'I don't think you should have made a promise like that.'

Her eyes glinted suddenly, and her chin lifted.

'Well, I have made it, and I intend to keep it!'

His eyes opened wide.

'Okay, keep it. I shan't try to dictate to you.' He brought a waiter to him with a wave of his hand. Jane drew a breath as she heard him order a double whisky.

'It's not good for you, Don,' she quivered. 'You used always to say too much drink was harmful.'

'I had nothing on my mind at that time. Don't worry too much,' he added, 'I'll be all right one day.'

'One day? How long is that?' He merely shrugged and she added, 'I hope you won't be going out every night, drinking.'

He set his mouth but made no comment, and again Jane changed the subject, asking him if he would do something about the tickets for their flight back to England.

'I'd like it to be soon—tomorrow if possible,' she added.

Don nodded in agreement, saying he would get Reception to phone the airport for him. Less than half an hour later they were booked for the late night flight the following day.

'We've been lucky,' Don said. 'They've had two cancellations.'

Jane sat back in the hired car, trying not to think, to have her will dominate her mind, instructing it not to work. If only she could sink into total oblivion, forgetting all that had passed in the last few months, and unable to see the terrors of the future. For there would be terrors. Don even now was much the worse for drink, but he had refused to let her drive. He'd get them to the airport safely and in plenty of time, he assured her. His mood seemed to change rapidly, from one moment to the next. After a short interlude of black despair he would begin to talk optimistically of their future together. Then within seconds he might be mentioning something about Gina—her hair was like gossamer, her skin like silk.

'She was beautiful—different colouring from yours. But she's gone and we've got to forget, haven't we, Jane—you as well as I?'

'Don, be careful!' The cry had left Jane's lips several times, before, exhausted by her fears, she had leant back, trying to put every thought out of her head. She closed her eyes, but her lids felt heavy and she opened them again.

And then it happened, swift as the crack of a balloon bursting; once moment the view was of a moving belt of road, golden in the headlights, shadowed at the sides; the next it was rising upwards to meet Jane's face, sinuous, like a writhing snake. She put up her hands to shut out the horror; the car spun dizzily; her head cracked against something hard and a cloud shut out the light ... the black cloud of oblivion.

Jane floated back to consciousness slowly, as if her body, carried on a breeze, was being gently brought back to earth. She lay still, staring up at something semi-dark, like the pleasant shade beneath a spreading oak tree. There were lights, too, like the sun when it filters through the branches. She turned her head, then moved her left arm; they both felt stiff, strange. Voices drifted to her, then there were figures which she was at first unable to focus, but when she did a little smile came and hovered on her lips.

'Philippe,' she murmured, then looked at the nurse.

'Only five minutes, Monsieur de Chameral—very sorry. Doctor's orders, not mine, as you know.'

'*Merci*—thank you, Nurse.'

'Philippe,' said Jane again, feeling her arm and discovering it was encased in plaster from just above the elbow down to the wrist. 'The car!' Suddenly she was fully alert, the dazed blissfulness of her senses shattered by memory stark and terrifying. 'We—we crashed, on the way to the airport. Don . . . is he in hospital too?'

Philippe was moving towards the bed, while the nurse drew back the curtains a little and the illusion of the sun through branches was dispelled.

'Jane darling, your husband is——' He turned as the nurse reached the door, a look of uncertainty in his eyes. She nodded.

'Yes, the doctor did say you could tell her.'

'I know, but——'

'Apart from shock, and the broken arm, she hasn't come to much harm at all. It's a miracle when you thing of it.' She went out. Jane watched the door close, then transferred her gaze to Philippe.

'Don's . . . dead, isn't he?'

'Yes,' answered Philippe simply, 'he is.'

Tears of pity welled up in her eyes.

'Poor Don,' she whispered huskily, 'poor, poor Don. So unhappy, torn apart by grief——' She stopped a moment and then, 'Of course you don't know it all——'

'He was not killed outright,' broke in Philippe gently. 'He lived for about two hours; he was fully conscious for the last forty-five minutes or so. He came to in here—in this hospital—and asked about you. When he was told that you would live he asked for me. He knew he hadn't long and he wanted to put everything right for you and me——' Philippe's throat seemed to become blocked for he swallowed over and over again before he was able to continue. 'There is nothing of importance that I do not know, Jane darling. Whatever he did to you once, and whatever he was ready to do in the future, he has at least done all he could to ensure your future happiness.' He seemed very moved, and Jane wondered what kind of a scene it was, at her husband's death bed, the poignant scene in which one man, coming to the end of his life, was determined to see that the other had a happy future before him.

She wept, turning her face into the pillow.

'Please don't misunderstand,' she begged even while being fully aware that the plea was unnecessary. Philippe understood the reason for her tears.

She felt his hand taking hers, his other on her brow. She turned, wincing at the pain in her neck but suspecting the injury causing it was nothing more than a bruise.

'I love you, Philippe,' she quivered. 'But all my thoughts are with him just for now.'

'I know, dearest, and that's how it should be. But try to remember that he's at peace, that the pain's all gone, for ever.'

She nodded, marvelling at his gentleness, his infinite understanding.

'I'll get well soon,' she promised, letting him dry her eyes with his handkerchief. 'And then—then I'll come home to you.'

'Home. . . . Yes, my beloved, you'll come home to me.'

★

It was a month later. Jane had been back at the chateau for three weeks, weeks of sadness as memories intruded, but of happiness as well for she and Philippe were together all the time, getting to know one another, loving and caring and planning for the future. They sat together in the twilight each evening, hands clasped, looking out across the lagoon and often never speaking a word until Meri or Rima came quietly to say that dinner was served. That there had been some gossip among the servants at the chateau was certain, but it could never touch either Jane or Philippe simply because it never came to their ears.

Don's body had been flown to England. Jane later wrote to his parents, expressing sympathy. They had known of the break, of course, but they would never know of the events which had occurred during his visit to Mauritius, for Jane had no intention of writing to them any more.

The children were in England, living in a rented cottage with their father and the girl who was soon to marry him. Mr Scott had sent photographs of the children with this young lady and one look at the sweet placid face was more than enough to bring all Jane's fears to an end. Although only twenty-six, the girl could not have children of her own and was delighted with the idea of a readymade family. Immediately they found a house she and Mr Scott would marry.

'Darling, what are you thinking about?' They were on the verandah as usual, waiting for dinner, when Philippe put the question, softly, his hand clasping Jane's tenderly in his.

She turned her head and a lovely smile broke.

'I'm thinking that all my troubles are disappearing fast—— In fact,' she added, 'I haven't a thing on my mind except, perhaps, a sad thought now and then for Don.'

'He's at peace, dear.'

'Yes, I know.' Her thoughts went to Yvette, who had, apparently, managed to get every detail from Don; and she had told it in turn to Philippe. As he had said, there was nothing of importance that he did not know, since what he hadn't heard from Yvette he had heard from the dying man—with the stories conflicting at times, he had told Jane. However, all was cleared up and Jane herself was not required to do any explaining at all.

Philippe had been all tenderness, but at first he seemed quite unable to throw off his feeling of guilt at condemning her out of hand.

'If only I had encouraged you to speak when you wanted to, I'd have known the truth....' She knew he was thinking of his words about there having to be one to speak the truth and one to understand it. 'Forgive me, my dearest, for mistrusting you. I said such terrible things——' Jane had stopped him, with a tender kiss and the simple reminder that it was all in the past and therefore it was not important now, when they were both looking forward to the future.

'Bless you, my darling,' he had said fervently, and from then on he had not mentioned it again, much to Jane's satisfaction and relief.

Jane herself had on one occasion mentioned all the lies she had told him, saying she did not know how he could forgive her. She had been stopped at once, with the stern injunction never to mention the matter again.

'I shall beat you if you do,' he had warned, and his face was so severe that she rather thought he meant it.

'Beloved, you are miles away again. I won't have it! Come back to me!' Once more his voice broke into her reverie and this time she promised not to let her mind wander any more.

'I was thinking of lots of things that have happened,' she confessed, snuggling close against his hard lithe body. They had risen, because Rima had appeared to tell them that the meal was ready to be served, but they had stayed a while, by the rail, looking out to the dark spread of the lagoon, and beyond to the twinkling lights of a ship out at sea. 'Oh, Philippe, I'm so happy I'm afraid!'

'Don't be afraid, my darling——' He drew her even closer, his arms like hawsers about her even while he was taking care to protect her injured arm. He bent his head, taking her eager lips in a long, possessive kiss. 'You must never be afraid of anything.'

She looked at him a moment later, when he took his mouth from hers. She saw the great tenderness in his eyes and a look of adoration illuminated hers. How she loved him! The sensation of caring so deeply was like wine in her blood, intoxicating, stirring the senses, sending her heart and mind to the realm of ecstasy that knows no rational thought or act. She said impulsively,

'I wish we were—together, Philippe.'

One brow was lifted in a gesture of mild amusement. 'Together, my love? And what are we now?' His eyes were on her face, flickering over it—from her soft rosy lips to her nose and eyes and forehead. His breath was a caress as he touched each feature with his lips, lingering with a sort of possessive arrogance, telling her that everything was his. 'It is more than this that you want?' He paused and laughed a trifle mockingly as she blushed. 'Brazen child,' he scolded. 'Shall I take you?'

Her colour deepened and she buried her face in his jacket.

'Dinner's ready,' she reminded him in a muffled voice.

For answer he swept her passionately into his arms, crushing her slender body, taking her lips, forcing them apart in a kiss that left her gasping for air.

'Dinner, my love, is unimportant!' His eyes were aflame with ardour, his hand on her breast possessive, almost painful, his hard virile frame excitingly warm as it melded with hers in close intimacy. 'You—darling! Dearest Jane, I adore you!' The tide of his passion swept her to the brink of heaven; she clung to him, every nerve craving for his love, for the fulfilment of this outpouring sensation of desire. 'When will you marry me?' he demanded when eventually, his ardour having cooled a little, he held her from him, his worshipful gaze on her lovely face, his hand now gentle on her breast, and infinitely tender in its caress. 'Under the circumstances, darling, I feel there is no need to wait.'

She agreed. It would be bordering on the hypocri-

tical to wait, pretending to comply with convention—
because both she and Philippe knew that it would only
be a pretence.

'In two weeks, then?' he said, his warm lips caressing the tender curve of her throat. 'Will you marry me
in two weeks' time?'

'Yes, Philippe,' she answered huskily, 'I'll marry
you then ... gladly.' A pause, but he seemed too
gripped by emotion to speak, and at length Jane went
on tiptoe to press her lips to his. 'Philippe ... dearest
Philippe, thank you for loving me.' Her voice was a
husky whisper, and her body quivered within the circle
of his arms.

'Dearly beloved,' he murmured as, with a sort of
savage tenderness, he brought her closer to his heart.

Harlequin Plus

A WORD ABOUT THE AUTHOR

Anne Hampson, one of Harlequin's most prolific writers, is the author of more than thirty Romances and thirty Presents. She holds the distinction of having written the first two Harlequin Presents, in 1973: *Gates of Steel* and *Master of Moonrock*.

Anne is also one of Harlequin's most widely traveled authors, her research leading her to ever new and exotic settings. And wherever she goes she takes copious notes, absorbs all she can about the flora and fauna and becomes completely involved with the people and their customs.

Anne taught school for four years before turning to writing full-time. Her outside interests include collecting antiques, rocks and fossils, and travel is one of her greatest pleasures—but only by ship; like many, she's afraid of flying.

What does she like most? "Sparkling streams, clear starry nights, the breeze on my face. Anything, in fact, that has to do with nature."

The bestselling epic saga of the Irish.
An intriguing and passionate story that spans 400 years.

FIRST...

The Defiant

Lady Elizabeth Hatton, highborn Englishwoman, was not above using her position to get what she wanted ... and more than anything in the world she wanted Rory O'Donnell, the fiery Irish rebel. But it was an alliance that promised only ruin....

THEN...

The Survivors

Against a turbulent background of political intrigue and royal corruption, the determined, passionate Shanna O'Hara searched for peace in her beloved but troubled Ireland. Meanwhile in England, hot-tempered Brenna Coke fought against a loveless marriage....

Readers rave about Harlequin romance fiction...

"I absolutely adore Harlequin romances!
They are fun and relaxing to read, and
each book provides a wonderful escape."
—N.E.,* Pacific Palisades, California

"Harlequin is the best in romantic reading."
—K.G., Philadelphia, Pennsylvania

"Harlequin romances give me a whole new
outlook on life."
—S.P., Mecosta, Michigan

"My praise for the warmth and adventure
your books bring into my life."
—D.F., Hicksville, New York

*Names available on request.